TESTAMENT
Collected Stories

TESTAMENT

&

Collected Stories

&

MOSES L. HOWARD

JUGUM PRESS

First print edition: August 2019
ISBN-13: 978-1939423962

Published by Jugum Press
505 Broadway East #237
Seattle, Washington 98102
Find ebook editions at www.jugumpress.net
Contact: jugumPress@outlook.com

CONTENTS

TESTAMENT
Collected Stories

HEATHER ON THE SURFBOARD

THEY CALLED ME A HOOKER in that newspaper article about teen dropouts. But I was never a prostitute. No way. It was because of my friend, Corkie, and how we watched the planes and fishing boats at Westport and Ocean Shores. That's where that stupid idea came from. Another reason was the police seeing me almost unconscious as though I was on some drug, when I was so seasick, I felt like I could die.

It all started with us watching the small planes that used to be up there in the sky like ships. If you looked at the clear blue sky where, on the horizon, the sky was an extension of the ocean. Looking up at it, you'd sometimes get lost in your thinking and not know for a time if you were on the ocean, land, or sky. I liked to feel that way, where you could imagine anything. Way up there, the planes sometimes looked like ships sailing in the ocean of the sky.

Those planes were up there on a clear day with the bright colors of white, blue, or red, the sun on their wings, and a glint of silver shining on their slick gliding shapes and flashing reflections on their windows when they turned, slowly catching the sun's rays, winking at you and flashing off the water below, near you, and the plane dipping toward you close enough for you to reach up and touch it. The plane kept coming in toward you at the shore where you walked or pushed your bike if you were tired of riding, or if you just dropped the handlebars to pick up a really cool seashell. The planes kept coming but never reaching land.

Their colors all red, brown, blue came in skimming over cottony clouds through the sky so clean, clear, and fresh. If you were in the right place, on the wide beach picking up sand dollars or trying to see what the ocean tides had washed up, you could see them land on the water with a big splash and skim over it a ways and stop and you were right there to see two or three people in the plane leaning out with goggles on their faces. You wondered why they stopped there. You wanted to know where they came from, where they'd go from here, and when they'd come again.

Because the planes always came back.

We could tell by the markings and numbers on them. Josh read the numbers, and he'd say, "Same as last week, Heather. I have those red numbers up here," and he'd tap the side of his head. They were the same planes. They came back after a day or two, or sometimes weeks. It was not an accident where they stopped, because we pedaled our bicycles along the beach there many times, and they always stopped in about the same place, as if it was marked somehow. Two or three people would be out there in a boat to meet them, and those on the plane came out on the boat and they talked and handed them the mail. That's what one of the men in the boat said to me and Josh and Corkie, when we asked them what the people in the planes did and what they brought. "They're bringing us mail and newspapers from other places."

"Something to sell in the stores at Westport?" Josh asked.

No, they said, it was just pieces of mail. We thought it was cool to have friends who visited you at the beach with airplanes that landed with boats under the plane.

I later found out they were not boats, but pontoons. I later found out lot of things. But I was no more a prostitute than a shell on the beach. That's all the three of us were, like shells on the beach. We roamed up and down it with the tides and the shore birds, leaving our toe prints in the soft, moist sand, feeling it under our feet and hearing the roar of the surf. Westport is so small, and there was hardly anything else to do. Nothing else to do. I didn't want to be home, even to sleep at night. I am going to tell you about that, but I was no prostitute or nothing like that then.

A few times we skipped school while our parents went to Hoquiam, Aberdeen or Olympia or Raymond or Tacoma or further, to Seattle, and we knew they wouldn't come right back. That wasn't often; we skipped maybe three times in three years. Those times, or when there was no school, like on holidays and long weekends, it was just me and Corkie and Josh. I am taller than Corkie, but she is more filled out and looks more mature. But she is not mentally mature. Although some men call her lady, she is really just a kid in many ways.

Almost every weekend we rode our bikes up along that wide stretch of beach above Westport, and sometimes we went to Ocean Shores if we could get a ride. I was in middle school. I am telling you about how we'd take our bikes and ride up the coast, and we'd spend the day in our bare feet, wading on the beach, lying nearly naked in the sand, or finding beautiful rocks and glass buoys and bottles. We'd hang our findings in a plastic bag from the carriage seat and if we got tired of riding, we'd find a nice warm stretch of beach with a log or sand grass and we'd empty our bags all in rows in the sand, to count and compare shells, white sand dollars, channel whelks, or buoys from as far away as Japan. We'd try to add up what we'd sell them for, or what we could get from tourists who came to charter salmon fishing boats.

Josh always held shells up to his ear to listen to the sound of surf. "How did it ever get in this here shell?" he'd asked.

But Corkie was kind of strange, claiming she heard people talking in the shells. She'd hold one to her ear and she'd almost pee her pants laughing and, I thought pretending; but she swore she heard people talking. She put a shell to my ear, asking, "Can't you hear them, Heather?" But I didn't hear anything and neither did Josh, except the roar of surf. She said it was a different language, that's why we didn't hear. She told us stories about the people she heard in the shell. That's one way that Corkie was strange sometimes. Maybe it was because her mother always needed money. I gave her a couple of my shells so she could sell them and have more money to take home.

Once I found this beautiful buoy of blue glass after the tide went out. It was almost buried in the sand among drying, green algae and twigs. I almost didn't see it, but then my toes rubbed the smooth glass and I knew I had found something great in the gritty sand. They said in town that it had floated all the way from Japan. I sold it to a tourist from Wisconsin for twenty-five dollars. That's how we made spending money, and we'd always share it. Tourists were looking for driftwood that had been washed clean and smoothed by sand. Sometimes it'd have shapes like animals or people. That was prized by tourists.

Don't think I'd ever dirty myself by prostituting. Washing in the ocean and walking on the beach allowed me to tolerate home. The thought of the fresh ocean waves washing over me made me feel fresh and alive. I just loved the ocean water over me. I used to wade out so far that I scared

Josh and Corkie, who'd yell at me. I'd hear them against the roar of the waves and wind.

"Heather, Heather, come back." That would be Corkie.

Then Josh: "Heather, are you nuts? You'd better come back. You're too far out."

But I was a strong swimmer and I was never scared, except when the big wave came in that time and took the man and his two kids wading in the shallows. They were not even far out, and the ocean was peaceful, they say. But a big wave came when they weren't paying attention and ran furiously up the beach, much higher than usual, and caught them by the legs and pulled them out. First the wave got the two children. And then this man, their dad, thought he could save them. He hopped in and tried to swim to them, but a second wave came in and it was very high, massively bigger than the one that got the kids, and pulled him out too. People just stared and ran away from the water's edge. It was so strange, because Josh and Corkie and I went down where people were standing about a half hour later, and the tide was going out. The waves were so small and quiet, no one would expect to be in danger. You'd never think that man and his children were out there, drowned.

Whenever anyone called me back, I never heeded them. I'd go so far out to meet those waves that they'd freak. "Heather, you better come on back now. I don't want to tell your momma you drowned."

Some tourists came by one day when I'd found this whale jaw that was washed white and clean. The teenaged son who was with them called it a baleen. He had to have it. The parents said yeah, go ahead and trade. He collected stuff like that. He said he didn't tell everybody, but he had a porpoise skeleton from when they lived in Hawaii, and he said he'd give me his surfboard. I had seen him try to ride waves. I told him he could have the old whale bone.

He also insisted on coming down for two sunny days to show me how to surf, but he always came out of the water shivering. He wasn't used to the cold, as he loved to say.

"Man, hey, it's colder than hell. It's down-right frigid," he said. "It's a goddamn refrigerator out here. It's way too cold, man. This thing I realize now is for Hawaii and California."

I gave him the baleen; he gave me the surfboard.

When it was warm I'd ride the waves like he showed me. I got good at it. I was used to the cold and could stand it longer than a warm tenderfoot from Hawaii. I'd go with the wave up, and it would engulf me. At its height I'd twist and separate myself from it and go on to its crest and in that way controlled my board. It was like nothing I have ever seen.

After that wherever I went, I took my surfboard on the back of my bicycle. I'd ride that surfboard through the waves until I was just laughing. I felt so clean. You see, if you kind of curved your legs so you made it raise along the crest of the waves, it's like being in a swing. You can kick the surf when you're up the highest, and then fling and turn when you feel the wave curling and go down with it. That's what I did. I did not pay any attention, but from time to time I'd see people watching and wondering about me.

When I surfed, I wore that old raggedly swimsuit that I bought in the Salvation Army thrift store. I'd duck down and scoop up water and wash everything off me. It felt just so good and my hair would be straggly, plastered down to my head. I was always glad we lived near the ocean, because I could wash anything off me, even dog shit and dog breath and the fumes of the stinking alcohol that my mom's boyfriend stunk up the closed house we lived in. My mom had lost my dad in the ocean, when a crab boat sank in Alaska. She came down to Westport, I think to be near boats and fishermen. I think she secretly hoped that he was not really dead, that he'd come in one day on one of the charter fishing boats that went out with tourists to catch salmon, since he'd lived in Westport before the Alaska job.

But it was Josh and Corkie and me who came in off one of those boats, with the police waiting for us after the Coast Guard escorted the boat in.

Mom loved these damn dogs, my dad's dogs, three of them. After he died, she kept them in the house wherever we lived. They always ate, whether or not we had a good meal. Since the house was always closed up, it stunk, because we had a house full of shitty dogs. It was all smeared on the floor, and you stepped in it if I didn't clean it up. Sometimes when she left, I took the hose and soap and sprayed everywhere, every damn thing in the house. I mean I washed shit and crud, the whole damn place. She was mad as hell, but by the time she started to raise hell, I had my bike and I was gone.

She was always sleeping with some crummy fisherman or another someone she met in one of the town's three bars, or on the dock where she went to pick them up, or as she scanned the ocean or just looked at the boats every day. The men had to be tall like my dad and have a tooth missing like he did and be strong from pulling nets or logging up at Forks. They'd talk and laugh and find they had something in common, and they tried to find it in her bed, laughing until all times of the night. They didn't seem to mind the stink in the house. I couldn't wait until morning. I could hardly breathe.

At the first light I'd run down to the beach and wash the night smells off me and wash up my nose and on my tongue with sea water. My clothes, the ones I'd wear to school, flapped and dried in the wind all night and smelled good the next morning, unless it rained. If that happened, I hung them under the shed of an old boathouse. It had an outlet, so I hooked up an iron out there on the table, and I used to iron my jeans.

By going out on the beach to watch that plane, we didn't know it but we were in danger. We didn't even know it when one of the men said to us once, "Why are you kids always here? Who sent you?" I thought that was strange. Why would anyone send us up the beach to watch a plane that nobody knew when it was coming?

But soon after that, when the guys met the plane in a motor boat, we were on the beach and a man was fishing from a little boat near the beach. When they left the plane, it took off. But something was wrong, because the plane blew up at the same time the motor boat did.

I saw the small boat go that way to help, but he just went quickly by, stopped for a short while, and then went off down the beach—I guess to report it, but we never saw the fisherman again. There was fire everywhere. While we were still watching and saying to each other that the men might've got off and were not hurt, the Coast Guard came. They went up and down the beach in their boats near where the plane had landed.

Another time shortly after that day, two men came. One of them asked us about the boat and if we saw it blow. We told him what we saw. He asked if we were the only ones around, and we said yes. We'd forgotten about the fisherman in the little boat.

Corkie didn't tell me about this, but after that, a guy asked Corkie if she wanted to sell some marijuana to people on a boat. Her mother was on welfare, and they always needed money because she had two small kids. Anyway, Corkie told him, "Yes," and did it without telling me or Josh. Before we knew it, she was "going out fishing." That's what she said.

She'd have on a life jacket. When people got seasick, she'd offer them Dramamine and she'd sell them marijuana, the ones that wanted it. Josh and I went out on the boat once, just to see what she was doing. We saw she was with one of the guys who'd been meeting the plane. One time a man came on the dock and just that guy. I was nearby, leaning out over the dock, and I heard him say under his breath, "Damn welcher." He ran away fast and hopped into a jeep. The Coast Guard was all over the place, and people started accusing Corkie of being a little prostitute who went out on the boats to sell sex. She had all this money and had thrown the marijuana overboard. They said she was a prostitute. Because I'd met her at the boat, we were questioned for hours by the police and some guy from the Coast Guard.

Somebody remembered me being taken off the boat the time I went out. I was so seasick, my clothes were hanging off me like I was drunk or had been attacked. Some old people remembered that and told it to the reporters, and they put the story together as they liked it. Kid prostitutes at Westport. It made a big sensation. The newspapers had reporters there talking to us and the police.

They didn't know what to make of it and never connected it to the airplane and the boat, but I think I could do a better job as a detective than any of them. They said that we both were hookers, selling our bodies to boatmen and tourist fishermen, and that Josh was no better than a pimp, telling the fishermen we were for sale. Somebody from the Seattle papers wrote that, but it was a lie.

I knew I couldn't live in Ocean Shores or Westport any longer, so I took my overnight case and caught a ride to Seattle to live with Aunt Amy in Fremont. I'm still scared, and I stay away from Corkie. I think she could still be killed. What happened to her when she came off that fishing boat is connected to that plane and boat that blew up in the water off Westport. I still wonder about that guy who was fishing, who went to the place where the boat and plane exploded, then disappeared. What was all of that about? Why hasn't the Coast Guard spoken to him? But we were never prostitutes. And Josh doesn't know the meaning of the word pimp. It's all a crazy lie.

I wrote to my mom, telling her to send me my surfboard. I sure miss surfing. Someday I may go to Hawaii or California, and I'll take my surfboard with me.

THE GEOMETRY LESSON

WHEN SHE HEARD THE SIRENS, Christy Finston was sitting in the hall with Danielle, studying for the geometry test that Olson was giving the next day. She was worried that the teacher thought she cheated on the last exam. She was determined to know the theorems, sides, angles, and proofs by heart on this test, so her eyes wouldn't stray, and she'd feel comfortable asking him for a letter of reference for college.

From her seat, through the window, Christy watched fire trucks skid to a stop right across the street. Police cars wheeled into the street, parking across it, cordoning off several blocks. Policemen rushed into the burning building amid people who ran in different directions. They accosted some, snapping on handcuffs. Helmeted firemen dragged over high-pressured hoses, spewing water, sending fountains of spray over the building.

Christy recognized students mixed in with neighborhood residents, moving hurriedly through lanes beside the school building to escape the police. Several of them, hands cuffed behind their backs, sat on the sidewalk; others were herded into squad cars.

Danielle texted and twittered on her cell phone until a friend suggested the fire was set by drug sellers, "targeting those who didn't pay."

The firemen put out the fire. The police in their cars drove away the arrested people. Christy went to math class, finding a strange girl sitting in her seat. The girl had black hair and was wearing a low-hanging purse with a strap over her shoulder. She only stayed a minute. Christy guessed she was in the wrong class. The math period was almost over when Tom Olson, the math teacher, came in and started to review for the test. The girl walked right past him and didn't say anything.

Christy needed to make a good grade on this test. She wanted Olson to know she was honest so he'd give her a good reference. She asked him right away.

"May we know the actual theorems you are going to emphasize on this test?"

As he turned to answer her, a student from the principal's office came for him. He excused himself. She decided to study, but when Mr. Olson left, there was only Danielle, Shaun, and herself in the classroom. The others had skipped.

Shaun said, "Class is over. What are we sitting here for?"

Without looking, Christy grabbed for her backpack. She pulled her geometry book and notebook toward her while unzipping that backpack. A calculator and stacks of money slid from the backpack onto the table. It wasn't her backpack.

Christy was startled. She looked around to see if the others had seen the money on the table. They hadn't noticed. She quickly stuffed a big wad of the money in her fanny pack, while she kept her eyes on Shaun and Danielle. She snapped the fanny pack around her waist. Then to draw their attention, she dropped the calculator and the backpack on the floor. The calculator made a loud clack, and the money cascaded out. Danielle and Shaun looked up and saw everything at the same time. Danielle gasped, her hand flew to her mouth,

"Oh, ho, Christy what's that all about?" They both ran over to Christy.

"Where did you get that?" Shaun whistled. "Somebody's hella rich."

Christy threw up both hands. "It's not my backpack."

The three of them crowded around the backpack. Christy looked around for hers. Someone had taken it, or she'd left it someplace else. She zipped the backpack up. The money was still on the table and floor.

Shaun came closer, looking at Christy suspiciously, his eyes darting toward the door and back to the pile of money. Danielle was already next to Christy, breathing hard. Some bills lay exposed on the floor; hundreds and twenties covered the table.

Shaun's eyes bugged out; they were enormous, gazing at the money. His voice kind of screeched and piped out in a whisper. "Whose backpack is it, Christy?

Christy stretched out her hands. She felt like an idiot, repeating what she'd said before. "I don't know. I thought it was mine. Then I opened it and all of that stuff flew out."

"Isn't there a wallet or something in it? Any ID?" Shaun asked.

Danielle said, "Yeah, we should find out whose it is."

Christy said again, "I don't know and I don't like this at all." Her hands were shaking. She felt a chill go down her back, and all kinds of thoughts ran through her head. Like, 'Could she get shot?' 'How will this get her in trouble?' She wanted to be somewhere else. She picked up her books, pushing past the table, leaving the backpack and money on it, and started for the door.

Shaun said, "No, Christy. You can't leave it just like that."

"I'm going to the office to get Mr. Olson. I don't want to be blamed for anything."

"But leaving just like that, who knows, somebody may come in and take the bag and you'll be in some kind of trouble. Besides, I don't want to be left with it."

"Wait," Danielle said. "Look! Hundred dollars bills! No telling how much is here. Open the backpack. See who it belongs to. We can put the stuff back and take it to the office."

Christy said, "Let's make a list of what's in it, sign it, and take the bag to the office."

They agreed. Christy saw they were excited and scared. Their eyes big, their hands trembling, and voices sounding strange.

Shaun said, "Lock the door while we are looking in it." Christy saw several people pass the window and she didn't want to have to explain the money to any students that just popped in. Shaun locked the door and Danielle closed the blinds.

With trembling hands and keen ears, Christy helped them lay out the stuff from the backpack on a table. They counted the money. Three stacks, two of which were wrapped around with rubber bands. One stack had tens, fives, and a lot of ones. There was $723 in that stack. There was a big stack with one rubber band around hundreds and another rubber band around twenties. They counted sixty-one twenties and two hundred hundred-dollar bills, close to $2,200 total.

Shaun said, "You know what I'm thinking?" His hands were not steady; his voice trembled.

Christy said, "We need to write down what we've got. Then let's see what else is here." She put a band around the money. In another little zip pouch, there was a bong and small plastic bags of brown chronic.

Shaun said, "I want that. Nobody is going to miss it."

Christy didn't say anything. She set it aside. Danielle was writing. She listed the money, a pack of cigarettes, a lighter, some wrapped Kleenex, and three chocolate chip cookies.

"You can have those, Shaun. You're so greedy for people's stuff."

There were breath mints, a pair of briefs that could be a woman's or man's. There was no ID, not even a scrap of paper. But there was a bus schedule booklet, a notepad, a ballpoint pen, and a candy wrapper.

Shaun had been quiet for a while. When they'd finished and started putting everything back into the backpack, he was breathing hard and excited again.

"You know what I'm thinking?"

Nobody said anything. Christy kept putting the stuff in the bag. She was anxious to get out. Shaun went on, his eyes narrow now.

"We could take a little bit for ourselves, or all of it. Nobody will ever know we took it. It doesn't belong to anyone. We could just trust each other and go for it."

"Let's do that," Danielle said. "It probably belongs to the people the police arrested."

"Do you want them to come looking for it and kill your stupid asses?" Christy said. "Look at all that money. People are crazy when you take their money. I am going to turn it into the office, and I want you guys to come with me. We are going to give it to the principal. I have parents at home and a baby sister. I don't want anyone coming to my house and killing everybody. It has been done before. I read it in the *Seattle Times*."

But Danielle said, "You know, Christy, he's right. We found the money. Turning it in, we don't even get any kind of reward. That's not right either. See?"

Christy said, "Is that what you want? A reward?"

Shaun and Danielle both nodded and agreed. "Yes, we want a reward, because once we turn it in, we're never going to get even a thank you."

Christy paused as if thinking about that. Then she said, "What would you consider a reward to be? How much?"

"At least twenty," said Danielle, "but I know old greedy Shaun will say, 'Twenty is nothing.'"

"Look at all this money we are rescuing for them," Shaun said.

"How much are you thinking then?" Christy said.

"How about a hundred? Is that enough not to ever mention it again, and we don't have to count it over? We can just tear up our note and give the entire bag to the principal, and it's his problem."

"Yes, that's what we want to do," Danielle said.

Christy said, "Okay." She took the money and gave each of them a one-hundred-dollar reward.

"We could get more," Shaun said, his tongue licking his lips, eyes all shifty. "We could get a lot more. It's our chance!"

Christy took her hundred and put it in her geometry book. She said, "I'm going to the principal's office right now."

Shaun said, "Just think about it a little."

"Let's think about it on the way to the office."

In the office the principal sat in conference with Tom Olson and a police officer. Christy, Shaun, and Danielle explained everything and gave the principal the backpack while Olson and the officer looked on. The principal looked from the students to Tom Olson, who shrugged. The principal shook his head and said, "We now take charge of it. We will let people know we have it. If nobody claims it, then it will belong to you finders or to the school. Thank you for your honesty."

Christy then remembered she'd left her own backpack in the art room. She raced to get it and catch her bus.

Christy took a seat near the middle of the bus. She hugged herself and pulled her fanny pack close to her face, feeling the big roll of bills. She was about to see just how much she had, when she looked out the window and saw Tom Olson in line to board the bus. She quickly put the fanny pack on her seat and sat on it. He usually caught this bus and was in line behind several noisy, frolicking students boarding the bus. The pushing, jostling, and loud jokes joined with the blare of horns, the squeal of tires on concrete, and the patter of running feet. He was last in line.

But now, what was this? Christy saw an unwanted sight. Hurrying, trying to get in front of him, was that same dark-haired girl who was in Christy's seat in Olson's classroom. Christy raised up momentarily to get a better look outside. It was that girl with the low-hanging purse, in high-topped shoes, jaws attacking the gum in her narrow cheeks. Now she stepped behind Olson. She moved about as if she was anxious to get on. She attempted several times to step in front of Olson. He discouraged it by cautiously raising an elbow in denial. When his coins jangled in the fare box and he started down the aisle, Christy acted as if she still had not taken any notice of anything around her. She opened her blue art book and began flipping pages with great concentration.

"Pine Street next," the bus driver called out. He kept up friendly chatter with passengers as they entered or left the bus. "We're on our way to the Paramount Theater, three blocks down!" the driver announced. The bus lurched forward and Tom, caught off balance, swayed in the aisle, catching the handrail near Christy's seat. She was still intent on her book, showing she was interested and committed enough to study on the ride from Seattle to Tacoma. Maybe after this next test in math his memory of her eyes roaming to other papers would be erased. Maybe during the commute, he might have a chance to give her some help on the test as she'd asked a question in class that he had not had time to answer, because of the police raid in the building across from his classroom. But then here came that dark-haired girl.

As Olson neared Christy's seat, the dark-haired girl pushed by him, and, swaying with the bus's motion, sat down beside Christy.

Christy sensed by the looks they exchanged that Tom Olson and the girl recognized each other. The girl would remember Tom as the teacher, while Tom would remember her as the girl who was briefly in the room. Neither spoke. The girl pushed rudely in beside Christy and began asking questions. Her loud, gruff manner drew the attention of an older woman who wore a hat and opened her eyes and mouth wide in disapproval. The girl's abrupt invasion of Christy's space displaced a backpack, which fell to the floor. One book broke free and slid out into the aisle.

This caused Christy to rise a little way from her seat to see where it went. Christy saw Tom watching her. She quickly sat back down. The girl paid no attention to the backpack or the books. Tom picked up the loose book and held it.

"Were you in that classroom near the street?" the girl said, leaning close to Christy's face.

Christy leaned away, toward the window. "Which street?"

"You know! I know you see what I'm saying. I don't want to make trouble for you. Weren't you there?"

Christy looked at her blankly.

"Let me break it down for you. It was a math class. See, over from where the people were running from the fire and the police… in the school building, the room next to where the cops had people cuffed in the street."

"I don't know what room you're…talking…"

"Oh yes, you know what I am talking about. I'm going to have to kick some ass." She looked around then. "He was there." She pointed a shaky finger at Tom. "You!" Then her focus shifted. "What's that?" She turned to the backpack near Tom's feet. "Where is my backpack?"

"You lost your backpack?" Tom offered. "Well, I'm..."

Christy broke in. "Why do you come asking me...?"

"You are a damned liar. You're trying to get me in trouble." The girl raised her voice. Her darting eyes must have caught sight of heads pointing in her direction, especially the old man with a knobby walking stick and the open-mouth woman in the hat, who continued to look and listen. The girl lowered her head and her voice.

Tom watched Christy and the dark-haired girl. Christy thought he saw the effect of the heat of the sun through the glass window and the hot breath of this girl flashing fully on Christy's face and neck, leaving a dull red glow on her skin, and pulling sweat from her pores. Christy squirmed, frowned, and put her hand up as a signal: this girl was too close. It was too hot in the bus. She tried to turn in the seat and only succeeded in moving her shoulders.

"But you know. I can...I will cause you some hurt if..." The girl threatened lamely. She turned toward Tom and the backpack in the aisle. "Mister, give me that. Is that this girl's backpack?"

Tom said, "What is it you want? What are you upset over? Try the school's lost and found." He looked from her to Christy. "Did you have something valuable because..."

"Just hand that to me, mister," the girl said calmly, but she was glancing around as if she wanted to take the bag and make an escape.

Tom said, "Some students handed in a backpack this evening. It's been turned over to the police by now. You can claim it. You have to prove ownership by identifying the contents..."

"To...the police?" The girl stammered, unbelievingly.

"Yes, it came from my classroom."

"Oh, hell," she shouted. "Then I am fucked."

This bus had only one more stop before it entered the freeway. It wouldn't stop again until it arrived in Tacoma, forty-five minutes later. Tom looked straight at the girl. "You were in my classroom. What was in the backpack? Identify the contents, and it's yours. You can claim it."

"What do you take me for? I can't go to no police. I don't believe you."

"Wait and I'll prove it." He took out his cell phone and started to dial.

"Hey, what are you doing? Are you calling the cops?" She jumped up from the seat.

"I am calling the school. You can talk to the principal who had the backpack."

In a minute he said into the phone, "Yes. Hello, Mark. This is Tom Olson. I have a young woman here who wants to know about the backpack. The one the students handed in today."

He handed the phone to the girl, who took it reluctantly as though she thought it was a trap. "Yep, about that backpack…that was my backpack. What…My name? My name is Donna. Yes, Donna Eagleton. No, I am not a student. Do you have it? I want to come and get it…I said I want to come and get it. Yes, when I get there, I can tell you what's in it. Yes, I know it has money in it. I am not telling you right now how much is there. What? Son of a bitch! I…I…I have to talk to the police? You handed it to them? Oh shit! This gets more fucked up every goddamn minute. No… no, not well. You wait and see. There are others who know how to handle you. I'll send someone to deal with you bastards."

She threw the phone back to Tom Olson. And it looked like she was going to cry. Her whole body shook. Her hands flew up to her face. Then she rocked from side to side. "I'm dead…dead! I am going to die…They'll kill me," she whimpered.

The bus slowed, then stopped. Christy noticed the light ahead was red and there was the crunch of brakes and somebody outside on the street yelled, "Just wait," and again, "Wait, can't you see I am trying to cross?" More people pushed their way onto the bus.

"That's my backpack and he's…" Christy pointed at Tom. "That's Mr. Olson, my math teacher. You can see now. We don't have your backpack."

The girl jumped up. "I got to see what's in that backpack." She desperately snatched it from Tom. The passenger with the knobbed walking stick, and who wore house shoes, opened his mouth wide and yawned.

The bus driver slowed the bus. Looking back over his shoulder, he said "Is there trouble back there?" No one answered him, but the girl sat down and searched hurriedly through the backpack's contents, throwing papers, lipsticks, combs, a crumpled cigarette package, and Christy's gym clothes to the floor.

"Oh, damn it! All you got is your school shit. It's not here. Nothing's here…not a damn thing. I'm in a heap of fucking trouble. I know you were in that room. I saw you there!" Her hateful eyes blazed back at Christy.

She looked at Tom, who sat quietly and sternly as the bus lurched through traffic. The driver called, "Spokane Street, last stop in Seattle coming up. Next stop, Tacoma Dome Station Park and Ride."

The girl threw the backpack on the floor, along with Christy's books, and as the bus came to its last Seattle stop, she snatched her cell phone from her purse and dialed a number. Said a few words, listened, then bolted. Ran to the exit and with a hateful glance back, jumped off the bus.

She disappeared for an instant behind the bus. Then Christy saw her, threading her way through rushing traffic, cars braking for her, tires skidding, horns blaring.

Then the girl stood at the bus stop for the route back into Seattle. Wild-eyed, she was still talking into the cell phone and gesticulating in the air to an invisible someone at the other end of the line. Her head swiveled, looking toward downtown and then looking after the bus as though she wanted to get back on and didn't quite know what to do. She stared hard at the bus, took out a pen and wrote something. The bus took off through the green light, made its turn and, with a loud grasp of gears, gained speed and raced steadily toward the freeway.

Christy sat for a moment shaking all over. After a while she got up snapped on her fanny pack and stuffed her things into her backpack, with the help of the silent old woman who had witnessed the whole thing.

Tom still held Christy's book. He looked down and tried to close it. But it wouldn't close completely. It bulged with papers wedged between pages. He looked at the papers, which proved to be a small *TV Guide*. But on top of that was money, a hundred-dollar bill. Christy looked steadily at him, unmoving. He handed her the book with a puzzled look.

Her hands shook. "We each took a reward for finding it."

Tom Olson paused a second. Then he sat back down.

Paint Spill

"Yes, Shana can do that," my mother said.

I heard her in the living room where she sat talking with two neighbor women. They never asked me anything. That's the way it always works. "Shana can do that," if they asked for a babysitter. Mother isn't mean or anything. She explained that we needed money. She's a single mother with two children, and I should help out when I can.

I was at the kitchen table doing my homework. Donnel, my brother, was in my mother's bedroom, watching TV. I chased him out, because he had a homework paper to do. I saw it in his backpack. He gets things over on Mother because she loves him so. It's almost like he's taken Dad's place as man of the house. He gets his way. Imagine, lying on her bed, watching TV—on a school night!

"Yes, Shana can stand with them until the bus comes. Then she can go on to her school," Mother said.

She was talking with two neighbors who lived in the apartments next door. They found jobs and needed me to watch their two kids until the bus takes them to school. Pamela, the heavier blonde one, had a seven-year-old named Peter, and the slim brown-haired one, Cindy, had an eight-year-old daughter, Kelli. I babysat them sometimes. They were all right, easy to manage indoors, but like Donnel, they showed different behavior waiting at the bus stop. They threw down their backpacks, circled around the street lampposts, and dodged about as though they'd dart out in front of passing cars.

"Donnel takes the same bus," Mother kept talking. "And she has to watch Donnel. It's no trouble for her to watch two more."

No trouble? She had no idea of the trouble, especially since the Paint Spill. A paint delivery truck crashed into a lamp post while trying to make a sharp curve and avoid a school bus. The truck turned over, spilling paint in the street. The city's crew cleaned the street, but the paint ran into the gutters, and now fumes rose up and passing pedestrians grabbed their noses as they walked by. But these kids loved that smell. They stood over the open drain and sniffed it.

"Come on! Get away from there, Donnel. If you don't get your little, silly self away, I'm telling Mother." I had to chase and yell at him every day.

I had to keep telling him—all of them. Eventually I was in charge of a whole bunch of these little kids. They were kindergartners through fourth graders. When my mother told those two neighbors that I was available, I got more kids every week. Mother added more, always with the phrase, "Shana, we need a few extra dollars."

Now, I was in charge of about seven of these kids. Every morning we headed for their bus stop, one block away, and it was my job to stand out there with them until the bus came, see them loaded, and then I could go to school. I'm always late because of that. I explained it to my school principal. It had happened every day for almost two weeks. I was fuming because I am a senior, and I miss a lot of class time.

But I was also worried about the kids huffing the paint fumes. If they kept it up, those little kids would soon be dope addicts, if they weren't already. I reported it to Mother, and they should have called the City to clean it up.

The principal didn't believe me when I told him. I took a note from Mother, but he thought I had written it. Adults don't believe the truth. I told him to come and see for himself. He should see where it ran into the gutters and overflowed into the drains all along our street from when that paint truck turned over two weeks before. The paint had dried and hardened, but you could smell the strong fumes rising from the drains. How fortunate no kids were hurt in the accident, but now the children were sniffing and huffing the fumes. He said something about it not happening on the school grounds and it was not his problem.

I said, "I'm late for school, because I'm herding children every day."

He looked at his watch and said, "Shana! Shana! Shana!" as if I was a special problem to him.

I told Mother that the children were out of control sniffing and huffing it. I heard her tell the mothers about it one night while I was doing homework, but none of them did anything. They did not even come out in the morning to see what was going on.

I asked the bus driver if he could change the bus stop for where to pick up the kids. You know, move it a block up away from the spill until the paint was cleared away. "Could you park and pick up students a block further up the street, near the post office?" I explained to him how the children were inhaling the paint fumes. He mumbled something about rules being set by the bus company and the City and waved me away.

Every morning they came down the street, racing to get to that gutter and drain. They stood over the drain, or by it, and breathed in, eyes closed and chests rising up and down. Then they whirled themselves around. It was like the playground to them. They acted like they were on the swings or monkey bars or something. They spun around and around no matter how I yelled. I dropped my book in paint, reaching for Donnel. He wanted to hold the book. I pushed him away and he went back to hover over the drain. Once he almost lost his balance. He was all giggly and laughing and wouldn't leave it. When I pulled him away, he got angry, saying, "Everybody else is there. Leave me alone."

I didn't know what to do. I stood watching, feeling helpless. When the bus came that day, I knew the driver would have trouble with the kids. For some reason they'd begun arriving at the bus stop a few minutes earlier than usual. That bothered me, because they'd have more time there, and I had noticed the more time they had, the more they seemed not to listen to what I said. They had not heeded any word I had given them for a day or two, and now they paid no attention to the bus's arrival. I shouted at them. They ignored my calling. Most of them wouldn't move away from smelling the stuff coming up from the drains.

I hurried among them, touching them, trying to persuade them, but they wouldn't get on the bus. I kept telling them the bus had a schedule, "Look you are delaying the driver." They didn't listen. They didn't board. They'd been doing this for two days, but today it was worse; they were out of control. I was also worried about being late for my speech class. I had to make a presentation that day.

I was confused and really angry. That's why I ended up in juvenile hall. I started snatching their little asses and pushing and then throwing them on the bus. Donnel was first.

I said, "I have had enough of this shit. Get on the bus now!" And I just dragged him in past the driver, who was grimacing and looking me.

He was an old-ass, retarded type, and I didn't have time to say more to him. If he couldn't see the problem when this happened, although not quite as bad, every morning for nearly two weeks, it was useless to think he'd help. He was too dumb to understand. I know I used some rough language. I hear talk like this at the high school every day, but it was not my habit to use it. But today I had had enough. I mean, I was so, so frustrated. I'm telling the truth. I don't know what came over me.

I said, "Come here, you little bastards. Get your motherfucking asses on the goddamn bus, now."

And I grabbed any kid near me and slung them through the door. Cars were stopped behind the bus because the flag was up, and the red lights were blinking. And I saw some people on their cell phones talking, but that did not matter to me. One kid was running all around, slinging his backpack and trying to avoid my extended arms. I grabbed Elton and pinned him to the ground, grabbed his backpack, and shoved him in. I did the same to Cecile, a skinny blonde girl who knelt near the drain. When I looked around, both their mothers stood there, mouths open, yelling at me for abusing their children. It was their day off work. I tried to explain. I even asked the bus driver to explain, but the bus driver did not support me, and I could not explain anything to any of them. They didn't listen.

Soon a truant officer came up. He watched me for a while without coming over to see what was going on or without trying to find out what was happening. It's strange how everyone made up their minds about what was happening without approaching me. Nobody looked at the kids. They all stared at me, and these two mothers were in the truant officer's car pointing at me. The line of waiting cars behind the bus grew longer and longer. Horns blared.

I succeeded in herding all of the kids on the bus. When the driver drove away, I turned to pick up my books and go to school. But the police car came up, and they put me in the back seat and went over to talk to the truant officer and the mothers who'd called them. Everybody's mother was there but mine. The cops came back, and one of them got in the driver's seat and started driving me to jail. He said, on the way, "What substances have you been using, ma'am, and how long have you been using them?"

I said, "I am no *ma'am*. I am a senior in high school. Go check my school record."

He said, "I see," but he didn't check. "You had children of your own catching the school bus?" he asked. Just asking questions and ignoring my answers.

I looked at him and I couldn't see straight. I didn't say a word.

But I was so goddamn mad, I saw black. Everything was black. I was so mad my face felt tight at the temples, and I was crying and this snotty filmy, gunk ran from my nose, and I let it come out and fall anywhere. On the cop's old seat. And a few times, I sneezed, and stuff flew through the air, everywhere. I saw this cop, quickly take his hand off the steering wheel and shake it, while glancing sidewise at me. He wiped his hand on his shirt front and looked at me crazy-like. I sneezed and coughed. I had been inhaling the shit, and in a way, he was right, I had been taking it—just like the kids—everybody had. Even people in cars who passed the spill.

Think of those little children. No one cared. I knew it was useless to try to do anything, because nobody listened or thought about what they saw. It didn't matter what my mother said, I'd never bother about those kids again. If I had to watch kids again, I'd just not bother. I'd look off down the street somewhere. Those other mothers could just go straight to hell. They shouldn't bother about their kids either. A lot of good it'd do them to care, because they couldn't watch and think. I knew no one who could see clearly or think straight about what is happening all around us.

ENRIQUE

I HAVE JUST COME FROM Mr. Evans, the counselor's office. He notices and comments on everything. He was watching my hands move around and how I am always running my tongue across my lips, and he says my eyes dance about, my shoulders move, and I clench my fist when I'm excited. But this isn't about me, it is all about my father. I have problems with him all the time.

Yeah I have poor attendance, but this time it's because I was locked up for the same reason that I have if I am ever in trouble with the law. I love to take OPCs. What's OPCs? That stands for Other Peoples' Cars.

I left home when I was twelve and I just followed whatever I wanted. He tried to beat me for borrowing a car. I reported him and he got in trouble. Parents aren't supposed to beat their kids.

There are members of my family all over Washington—my uncles, aunts, and my cousins. When my dad gets all bossy, I go to visit them, one family or the other. They understand me and they say Enrique, you need to grow up, man you can't always act like this. But they let me stay around them and they don't hassle me much. If they do I move on. I have other relatives who will let me stay.

My father's brother Alberto is the worst though. He's like my father and calls me a bad example for his kids he's trying to raise. When I am around, they don't mind him as well as at other times. But he lets me stay around. I have always had problems with him and my father.

My mother is smart and beautiful, and she's got skills. I told her she should leave my dad. She could do better by herself, and I could take care of her. I don't know how she got with him. What did they ever do together? She knows three languages. I want to be like that. I am just getting settled again with my mother.

But my father never got along with me. It's his way or the freeway. He was born in Mexico. I am not talking against him, but this is America, the USA, and he is too old fashioned. He has got to lighten up. He can't get along with anybody. He had a chance back a few months ago to make big money, but he turned it down. He has money, and a guy told him if he bought a big truck, they could transport produce from Mexico and bring along a few people who couldn't get in the country otherwise. They could make a thousand bucks for everyone they brought with them. And my father blew his stack. He told the man to get away from him and his family, and he was just fuming and shaking with anger. He didn't want to know more, yet people are making a fortune helping migrant workers cross.

He fires a lot of people for getting drunk just once and not coming to work. He don't give nobody a chance. When you come to work for him, be ready to listen to a lot of rules. He meets with new workers and says, "I am telling you before it happens," like people are a bunch of babies.

He was a migrant farm worker himself. He and my mother worked very hard, and he got work in a print shop. He learned the whole thing by working at night. My mother told him to stop or he'd lose his health, but he worked, and now he owns the shop. He's lucky he ain't dead. But my mother has skills also. When he got the business and could pay for it, she went to school. Now they make good money together, and they send money back to my grandparents and sick relatives in Mexico.

They send too much. People there don't need it as much as we need it here. I could have a car with some of that money. I work for him now. I know the business and can do it as well as he can, but he doesn't trust me.

My mother is very smart and she works for the government. She is very beautiful, and he's telling her what to do and how to treat me. If she gives me a dime, he says she is helping me to maintain bad habits. He says I smoke her money away. I keep telling her she should leave him. We could live together. But she says he's my father and he loves us, and what we have is all because of him, and we have to learn to get along. All he thinks about are the cars and what I did in the past. I tell him I'm in school now.

And he says, "Why?"

I tell him, "Because I need to be."

And he says, "How many credits do you need to graduate?"

And I say, "Twenty."

"And how many do you have?"

I know I should have about fifteen credits already, but I have only six. I don't answer. He stops his presses and looks at me, like he's sorry. I can't answer. Holding his hands above, and looking straight at me with his full attention, he says, "Enrique, does anything meaningful and important ever make a dent in your hearing, or does it just pass over your head?"

I don't know what he's saying. Of course, I hear what is said to me. He is the one who doesn't listen.

I say to him, "I got skills. You know I've got skills."

He starts talking about the cars. "If you want to graduate, leave the cars alone." He's still looking at me. "Look, how old are you?

I don't say anything, and he says, "This is important for you to realize, and I don't know how else to tell you what your responsibility is. How old did you say?"

"Look, you know this. I am nineteen."

I can see his point, because I should have at least fifteen credits if I am going to graduate by the time I'm twenty. I see then it is almost impossible. I say well what do you suggest? And he's about to tell me something, but I got a point about what he just said about my not hearing, and I tell him about how I always listen to uncle Alberto and how he praised me for paying attention. I never took one OPC the last time I visited him. I go on talking about skills and so I let that moment pass. He goes back to his work, cleaning off the press with the little brush he keeps in his apron. He says over the noise of the machine, "If you don't go to school now, you'll be locked up. You're on probation. Do you realize that?"

"I know all of that," I tell him.

"Enrique." He stops the machine again.

This time he comes over to me where I'm standing near the door. He moves near, right next to me the way he used to do when I was little. I looked at him and there was something friendly and soft in his eyes, and I expected him to reach out his hand and tousled my hair the way he did when I was a kid. I saw him kind of move like that, and he said, "Son, you must always tell yourself the truth about what you know about yourself. The truth is, you've dodged responsibility, and now you've got to pay for that. They're making you go to school."

I had to swallow hard and look away, because he doesn't talk like that now since I have grown up. Anyway that moment passed, and he started up the presses again like our lives were being printed there.

I know a lot of stuff and if I've a mind to, I can do anything. I haven't been in school for two years but I have been learning. I have skills, and he is not the only one in my family. I have relatives all over. You know migrant workers move all over, and my dad brought other members of the family. You know, sent them money and told them legal ways to get in. So I got lots of family members. I was born in Pasco, and we lived in Sunnyside. Sometimes I go there, but I have relatives in California and Nevada.

I spend time in Mount Vernon. I just came from there. That's where I got in trouble with rowdies. I never had a driver's license in my life, but I am one of the best on the road. I can cover more miles, because I know when and where to do what. I have never owned a car. That's too much trouble to own your own car. But I have been driving OPCs as long as I can remember. I drive them and police don't stop me until I get a bunch of careless rowdies in the car with me who make a bunch of mistakes.

I drive OPCs and never get stopped unless some dummy does something silly. That's how I got on probation. Every time I've been in juvie or been locked up, it's somebody else who got me caught. I drove to Mount Vernon and had my own OPC for six months until I got tired of it and it needed a lot of things done to it. I couldn't take it to a garage to have it repaired. They'd have known by the VIN it was jacked, sure as hell. The police never knew it was stolen until I left it parked near a levee for a week. Then I saw they towed it. All the time I drove it, I was not stopped; not once. They came to my cousin's house. I was in the bed. They said they'd found a letter in the back of that car from some school in Seattle, and it had my name on it.

The car was stolen in Seattle, and did I know anything about it? I told them I didn't, but there was a gas ticket where I had bought gas. They took me to that gas station. The guy there said I had driven that car in several times to get gas. So I got busted. If it hadn't been for my rowdy cousins who worked in the fields, always talking and telling where they lived, the cops never would've known me. I am careful. I got skills. I can do a lot of stuff. You say I need to give every part of my life some thought. I do that and I come to the conclusion that I know more than some with diplomas and two-year degrees. I know some stuff they don't know. I make good decisions and I think Mr. Evans is all wet when he says people who smoke dope never know if they're making good decisions or not. Then he says, "Does that make sense?"

I say, "Hell, no. I always know what I am saying, whether it's right or wrong. How can a joint make you think wrong? A joint relaxes you, see."

You know I visit relatives all over, but I got skills and I'm no migrant worker. I tell my relatives that when I visit them. They know my father has his own business, and they know I don't work in the fields. I don't hoe tomatoes or cut cabbages. I don't pull onions or pick up potatoes. That's not for me. When I was little, I used to pick strawberries and pull apples, but I had to tell myself, "Hey, what are you doing? That's slave labor. Don't do it!" And now my relatives say, "Enrique, you know he's not going to do anything. Maybe he'll take you to a store or take you for tacos, but he ain't going to cut flowers or anything."

When I stopped working in the fields with my folks, my father said it wasn't anything wrong with working for a living. When I refused, he said I was stubborn and wanted to beat me, but the CPS says you don't have no right to abuse children. When he tried it, they came to arrest him. Same as they did when he beat me for stealing that first car. I stole the car, but they wanted to put him in jail for beating me to stop me from stealing. Ha, ha, don't you think that's funny? He's not even a criminal and they want to arrest him. Like the other kids here, nobody can put their hands on us. We got freedom. We're liberated. Hey!

I told this teacher, old Mr. Moore, "Hey, you're cool and all, but you make a lot of mistakes, more than me. Like yesterday morning when you kept asking James and me to stop talking during class. We were talking about the DNA lesson, but you wouldn't listen when we tried to explain. You separated us while other students were disrespecting you right under your long nose and you never said a word. I guess you are usually fair— that's what the other students think—but that wasn't cool. Don't even go there next time."

"Hey, wait, here comes Mr. Evans. Mr. Evan's cool."

"He's coming to ask me something."

"Enrique, have you had a chance to think about what we agreed about, that things don't seem to be working out with you and your father?"

"You got that right."

"Are you going to think about it and make some decisions that can improve your relationship?"

I just throw up my hands at that.

"I can't do anything. My mother should leave him. Just because he's got that printing thing, he doesn't listen to anybody."

"What about getting a GED? It will take you two and a half years, even going to summer school, to get a diploma. And you'll be over age in about a year."

"Mr. Evans, I just need to get off probation and I'll be all right. I already know a trade."

"If you get the GED, you could take a mechanic's course in one of the community colleges. You seem to like cars. A mechanic's certificate would get you a good salary."

"I don't like to work on cars. I like to drive them."

"How will you buy one to drive if you don't have a job? And you are on probation and must attend school anyway."

"I don't need to buy OPCs." I laughed in Mr. Evan's face. Jacinto, one of my friends, came up and high-fived me. "I don't need to buy. Others buy, I drive. What kind of car have you got, Mr. Evans?"

Both of us, me and Jacinto, know that Stanley Evans does not have a car. He commutes by bus.

Jacinto patted his pocket the way he does when he has stuff. I left Mr. Evans without making any decision about my father or school or anything and went out to Jacinto's car to smoke some bud.

INVISIBLE WOMAN

BRIAN CALLED ON TUESDAY, TWO days after I returned from a show of my recent sculptures in Paris. We laughed and flirted. I told him how excited I was to be back. We had lunch the next day at Harvey's in the East Village, a place we used to frequent when we were in university.

"What do you think of the idea for the party? Remember, I texted you about it when I was so busy that I could have dropped."

"Good idea. Where is it to be?"

"My studio. I thought I'd show off my new work."

I didn't say it to him at the time, but I had in mind showing him off, my boyfriend, and getting close to him at the same time.

"Who is invited? Who is coming then?" he asked.

"I thought we'd both chose. That way anybody we care about will be there."

"You mean we both can invite guests?"

I had not thought of it, but it sounded like a good idea. I'd get a chance to see who was in his present circle. That would be interesting, since I didn't know anyone interesting, as my whole life had been made up of artist types. We talked a little more, and it was understood that he'd invite Robert Moreland and Tina Schulte, and I'd invite Debra Irons. And I put Charlotte Long on my list. All friends from our college days.

I am Celeste Muldrow, the well-known sculptor. People see me as successful, but they never know how I got there. Now my pieces are outside banks and museums in Chicago, Denver, and eight other major cities in the United States. One is at the United Nations building in Oslo, Norway. But I still work in my loft studio in Denver, the Mile High city.

My life has been one of constant change and adjustment. It hasn't been easy.

Before I turned to sculpture, I was a painter and earned my living for years as an artist's model. I spent years posing without changing attitude or position while artists of lesser abilities transferred facsimiles of my image to canvases that sold. Artists often complimented me on my discipline and told me it came from my ability to suspend the moment and to put forth any emotional stance the artist asked me to portray.

Now that I was a success, I was bringing other aspects of my life into orbit. You see, I postponed love connections with the exception of Brian Weathers. We had this understanding since high school. He'd gone ahead with his rise in the business world, and now I was twenty-seven and he was thirty.

The party in my studio would give my friends a chance to become acquainted with my recent work, and it'd put Brian and me back out in social life together in what I hoped would lead to wedding bells.

My loft studio is one wide room. Guests entering it come first into my living area and there are no exit doors. I use my sculptures to divide living space from studio. The night of the party, I had it arranged so guests come directly in and find tables and chairs as they exit the elevators. The hors d'oeuvres and drinks and punches are all arrayed around on tables of the room. My sculptures of bust and full-length features form a life-like motif, where they all strike attitudes of real living people. I have one bust of an artist, another of a president, and several of current models all dressed in the latest styles.

As the guests began arriving, I stood near the opening of the big freight elevator and greeted them. I had a waiter from Harvey's serving the drinks. He bid them welcome all around and bade them survey the artistic pieces first, which they did. I noticed that Brian, Robert, and Debra Irons came as one party off the elevator. Robert lashed out with one of his jokes about not being able to distinguish the artist from her sculptured pieces. We all laughed. Debra and I had a girlie hug. She remarked, "Celeste, I like the way your dress hangs on you."

At that moment I did not appreciate the remark, for I was disappointed that she was among the party with Brian, who seemed all smiles. I hugged Brian and whispered in his ear. "Welcome, handsome."

He said kind of loudly, "This is a superb way to welcome you back into circulation."

I said, "I only want to circulate with you." Still whispering.

Soon after they went in, I saw Debra with her head close to Brian's, saying something that seemed private. They moved about and stopped where I'd placed several stands with little stages on the bottom onto which I intended to attach several life-size pieces for viewing later. Seeing them together like that I longed to hear what they were saying. They seemed too cozy. What would my party be like if I were not here? As an artist I always yearned for the real. Suddenly I realized that I knew how to make that happen. How I could disappear.

We had a three-piece band that performed calypso numbers, loud and distracting. It was a good thing I'd worn a grey dress. While all eyes were on the band, I whirled, placed myself in an immobile stance among the sculptured pieces near one of the empty stands and pulled a scarf from one of the couches and wound it around my arms and head as an artist's model. People passed, glanced but apparently did not recognize me as a living person. I was getting away with it like the human sculptures on the streets of European cities. I stood there in artist model mode, a part of the scenery.

Soon Debra and Brian came by, holding drinks, waving to people. Someone came up, spoke to them, and then drifted away. Debra craned her neck, whispering to Brian. She sneaked a kiss. "Where's Celeste?"

"She's making like a hostess."

She touched Brian's arm, leaning toward him. "Did you tell her yet?"

"No, there's been no chance."

"But you went to lunch with her."

"Deb, it was her first night back. I am not heartless."

"But if you don't tell her soon, she'll be the only one who doesn't know we're engaged."

I almost dropped off the pedestal stand, but I kept the pose together until the band came on again with one of their snappy numbers where almost everyone danced. And I came alive, moving with no one knowing the jolt my heart was taking. My first act was to brush away tears and to adjust to that surprise, while moving, watching, and joining the other guests, dancers on the floor among my art pieces.

I showed my professional model side to Brian and Debra, to all guests. In private, I was determined to work on the sculptured model, my life.

When Brian gets around to telling me the news, I wonder who will act surprised.

KAREN

KAREN AND I HAVE BEEN friends for twenty-nine years. Our friendship started when Seattle School District began busing kids around the city. I was teaching at Roxhill in West Seattle and many of our kids were bused to Dunlap in the south end.

That meant teachers from Roxhill were switched with their students to Dunlap. That was when I met Karen. She was a librarian and one of the teachers at Dunlap who accepted the new students and teachers and made us welcome. She was a librarian very interested in teaching students, and we did a project together, making books. I didn't know much about teaching elementary students. Karen knew a lot, so she shared that knowledge with me and we grew to be great friends.

Karen had lots of friends. She loved her work in the library and she was good at teaching kids. She loved to teach values, and she was always discovering new ways to do that. She was friendly, charming, and had a lovely infectious laugh. In the middle of all of this teaching and explaining, she always found something funny to share and enjoy with kids and other teachers.

One of her pet projects was the celebration of Martin Luther King's birthday. She wrote and directed school programs around his birthday and involved many students in the practice of tolerance, respect, and sharing. After an altercation on the playground I have heard students in the principal's office chiding another student. "Remember, we are supposed to go to school together and share and respect each other, and you didn't do it. And that caused the problem."

After Karen went back to University of Washington and got her degree in library media, she went to Alaska and worked in the Archives section of the University of Alaska.

She told me that she learned a lot there, but she missed the students and teaching values, and she thought the world needed more of that. When she came back, she began a different kind of intervention to teach values. She began examining the books that children had to read, and she held mock trials in library sessions with kids. She had kids as lawyers and judges and kids playing parts as characters from books. The actions of characters in books were examined, and some were accused of criminal activity. I remember specifically Jack and the Beanstalk. First Jack was censored for trading his mother's cow for a hand full of beans. What was he thinking of? Then for breaking and entering the giant's house and for stealing the goose that laid the golden egg. The giant was arrested and brought to court for threatening Jack with his *Fie fi fo fum I smell the blood of an Englishman.* The giant's timid wife was questioned about her silence when the giant threatened people. It was hilarious, it was educational, and the kids learned.

Karen used to play parts when she read books to kids. She became a character in the book she read to them, and the kids could never during that time address her by her real name. She wanted them to get into the story, to pretend. For example, if they called her Mrs. Jones, she'd say, "Pardon me, but I'm Jack's mother." Or, "Look, I'm the giant now. Listen."

I thought of this recently when she was laughing and telling me how she and Truman, her four-year-old nephew, had a play pillow fight. She was laughing while telling me of the pillow fight just as she used to laugh with kids in the library.

Karen was bipolar and for years had been in psychiatric care. She used to sometime forget to take her medication and end up in a health center. Often when she came out of a center, even before she went home, she stopped by the school where I was teaching. I'd be out of the room, on the playground or in the office, and when I came back, Karen would be there among my students, talking and teaching and having fun with them. It was all very natural for her to be there.

Karen loved her family and was always interrupting our visit to call to see where everybody was or what each member was doing. Or she'd give an account of which member of the family she'd just visited or was going to visit, or some drapes or something she was making for her brother's house.

Then twelve years ago, I got cancer. A lymphoma. Almost everyone thought I was going to die. The teachers at my school wanted to name a learning center after me. Karen was very sad, and she came to visit me. She knew I had a young son who was ten years old, and I spoke to her about not being able to see him graduate from high school. She thought about it and said, "Don't let them name a center after you. People do sometimes survive cancer. I really believe you will see your son graduate from high school." She was very serious. I could tell it by her voice. We all knew that Karen survived many things. She survived them with courage and often in good humor. I believed her. I went to the teachers and said, "Don't name a center after me. Buildings are named for dead people. I'm not dying." Karen visited and supported me through that.

Now it was Karen. She had cancer, lung cancer. I didn't know it, but this was her second time with it. Through our years of friendship, she'd always been a smoker. If we had lunch or dinner, she'd say immediately after, "Do you mind if I smoke?" I did mind. I hated smoking, but I loved Karen, and so I lied. I said, "No, go ahead," and she would smoke. Once I asked Karen, "What is it really that you get from a cigarette? Why do you smoke?" She thought about it, took a puff or two, and said, "Moses, a cigarette is like a friend."

It was her friend, the cigarette that killed her. Now she'd been given the news by an oncologist from the University of Washington medical team. If she didn't quit smoking, she would die. She tried. She tried lots of things, but she'd call me up and I'd sense that she wanted to tell me something I'd say, "Karen, how are you?" and she'd say, "Oh, you know I have smoked three cigarettes in five days," and then she was smoking again. She did not want to give up her friends, whether they were human or cigarettes.

She used to give me books that she thought might interest me. We both liked and shared reading the *New York Times* and dictionaries and encyclopedias. Any time no matter where we were, we'd go look up a word or an idea. Our idea of a good time together was a trip to a sandwich shop and the nearest library or bookstore. Recently we were looking up something in the encyclopedia. She reminded me of what the doctors predicted and said, "Moses, I am going to…would you like me to leave you my encyclopedias when I go?"

At the word "Go!" an alarm sounded somewhere inside me.

I heard something final in her voice, something that I didn't want to hear, something that shocked me. I came near to her and said, "Listen, I don't want your damned encyclopedias." I thought about all the times I'd watched her reading and acting and directing kids in her library. "If I can't look up words with you, I don't want to look them up at all. As a matter of fact, I'm thinking of leaving you my encyclopedias when I go."

TOOLS

PETER HATED TO FIGHT WITH Angela. It hurt him to upset her, because she took everything he said so literally, and she suffered if he made any statement that she could interpret as disparaging.

Last night he'd said, "I don't see why you make up scenarios on everything I say."

She said, "I listen to you, but you don't hear me."

"I do too listen and hear what you're saying. The problem is what you do with my answers."

"Maybe your answers aren't clear."

Peter looked at her as if she were joking, but she acted as if she really meant it. "Angela, you blame me for everything. What would life be like for you if you didn't have me to blame?" Peter got carried away and kept on talking. "What if you didn't have me? I mean what stories could you make up without me?"

As if she couldn't believe what she was hearing, she said, "What?"

Obviously, Peter should have stopped then and gone to mow the lawn or do something in the garage, but he kept talking. "What would you do if I didn't come home? You'd have no way to amuse yourself. I'll bet you're thinking you'd use surrogate ideas, but that wouldn't be like the real thing of blaming Peter."

She said, "You are kind of stuck on yourself, aren't you? No one is irreplaceable."

He asked, "What do you mean?" But she wouldn't elaborate. "What's your point?" He pressed her for a reply. It was a debate, and in a debate, you say what it is that defends your point.

"I was answering what you said, about no one could do without you."

"Meaning what?"

"I just said no one is irreplaceable."

"Are you thinking of replacing me?"

Angela looked directly at him, smiled a crooked smile, and turned away. She was repairing a towel dispenser in the kitchen cabinet that she'd complained to him about for nearly two weeks. He'd meant to get to it, but things kept getting in the way. Like he took the dog to the vet, waxed his car, and…

"I can fix that," he said, trying to coax her away. But she snapped it shut and then pulled out a towel and the thing dispensed.

"See that?" She pulled out another towel and handed it to him to wipe his hands, showing him that the dispenser was now working. Then she came up to him with both arms extended and said, "There are other things that you can fix."

He looked into her pretty grey eyes. His arms enfolded her warm curves, and he was sure they both fixed some things inside of them.

She pinched him and ran into her home office.

But things that seem to be fixed are just patched up and can go on needing to be really mended. Sometimes when arguments were over and everything seemed to be all right, they really were not fixed at all, and later he was in a kind of battle with a number of small skirmishes. None of which he clearly won.

During that evening, Peter saw Angela do a complex computer operation that she'd begged him weeks ago to show her. They never seemed to arrive at the computer when she had time to listen or he had time to help.

"How did you learn to do that?" he asked.

"We had a workshop at school one evening, and we all learned about networking."

Two nights later, Peter came into her work area and saw her flashing on the wall PowerPoint slides from a report she was presenting. She'd said a month ago, "We could learn PowerPoint together." Now she already knew it.

"How did you learn that?" Peter asked.

"Saturday class at the YWCA, "she said.

"I thought you went there to exercise."

"I do, but I am a multitasker. While I was there, I thought I'd just step in a class and watch. Then three weeks ago, I enrolled. Just forty-five minutes a week. It's fun!"

Peter went out to the lawn. With the slow spring rain, the grass quickly grew taller than Peter thought it should be. He needed to repair the lawn mower. It wouldn't start. She must have heard him in the garage tinkering with it all of that afternoon. Later when he came in to eat, the grass still was not cut. He left it like that for nearly a week.

Then on Thursday Peter took off early to repair the lawn mower. Angela was already home when he got there. She was in the garage workshop. She'd made sandwiches and tea as if she expected both of them to eat. How did she know he was coming home early?

Using a manual on small motors, she'd taken the lawnmower apart. A whole stack of tool magazines lay near her.

"You know, Peter," she said, handing him a sandwich and a cup of tea, "these motors are in almost every kind of appliance. They are in hair dryers, clippers, even the cooling fans in computer monitors. In every appliance, they're just a little different."

"How are they different?" He started to eat.

"They're covered over with plastic, but if you remove the right screw, like this…" She held up a screw between two manicured fingers. "You can reveal the working part. Look at this generator and filter." She pointed to the mower motor's dismantled parts. "I tightened this wire and washed the filter with gasoline, the way the manual recommends. Now let's see if it starts."

He was looking at her beautiful hands and body in amazement.

She put the lawnmower back together and hit the primer button three times. He heard a gurgling, like a mechanical swallowing in the machine. She jiggled the spark plug cable. It sounded like rough pieces of sandpaper moving over each other. *Wheeze, wheeze.* She reached over and pulled sharply on the start handle. The motor issued a soft, irritable answer like a noncommittal growl from a small dog. It sputtered twice and sprung into alternate barks and growls until it attained a constant roaring rhythm. They both stood listening to its smooth sound. She grasped the handle of the lawn mower and ran it down to cut a clean, clear swath in the green lawn, like a clipper moving effortless through a young boy's hair. She clicked the motor off and put her arms around him.

Peter thought she was wonderful. Perhaps this was the time to settle that issue still hanging over their blissful marriage. He revived that argument so he could fix it.

"You remember what you said the last time we argued and you were angry?"

"What?" she said, not even looking at him.

"You remember that crack about no one was irreplaceable."

"I never said anything like that."

"But you did."

"I don't remember it. I thought we were debating. Whatever I said was to refute your point. I was never angry about it."

"You said that," he insisted.

"Why do you bring it up now?" She was smiling, teasing. And there were those beautiful grey eyes again, and his heart kind of leapt up with love and admiration.

He thought it better to drop it, so he finished mowing the lawn. He mowed, admitting to himself that Angela was both smart and beautiful. In playing around and talking about almost anything with her, he'd always alluded to or told her how beautiful she was. Somehow he never thought it'd be helpful to praise her intelligence, for he knew she was the smartest member of the marriage. So he just told her she was cute and he loved her. He never said, "You're smart to figure that out." He wondered now if he should say that. It was the truth. But he kept mowing while she pruned a shrub.

When he went into the garage to put away the lawn mower, there was that stack of magazines on the counter. They were all from tool companies or they were about tools. One magazine caught his attention. The title: *10,000 Tools—A Tool for Every Job*. He thumbed through it and it listed all kinds of mechanical tools. He marked the pages of a few that he intended to buy, then he leafed through to the back inside cover. There were listed other magazines extolling the values of each magazine and the importance of other kinds of tools. He read down the list: plumbing tools, garden tools, software tools, sex tools, housewife tools. Peter noticed there was a fresh check mark beside garden tools, software tools, and sex tools. He looked up meaning to ask Angela about what she intended to order, but she was somewhere in the backyard.

He was worried then. He had the feeling that Angela had really decided to make him obsolete. If she gets a tool for every possible job, including sex tools (he had a too-vivid image), she could replace him. His throat felt dry. He rubbed his hand over his head and eyes. Was their marriage in jeopardy? He didn't know what to do. He felt a sudden weight in his chest. It was hot in the garage. He had to have some ice water.

In the kitchen he spilled ice cubes and water on the floor. And before he could wipe it up, Angela was beside him with this special spill mop. It was new and very effective. She whisked the floor twice and the water was gone, and so was she, outside again, pruning. How did she know he was in the house? Did she have a monitoring tool that told her his every move? It was something that he couldn't talk to her about. He simply had to watch her take over his functions as a husband by replacing him with tools.

From then on he thought a lot about their house. He found things that needed to be done and came home early from work and did them. One day he edged the lawn and replaced a leaky faucet in the bathroom. The next day he repaired a window latch and changed the cartridge in her fax machine. The next week he took apart the fans and cleaned the blades. Then he had her car oiled and serviced on his day off. He did everything, trying to make sure she had no need for tools.

He thought he should be up to date, so he stopped in at the library on Tuesday and spent an hour with the *Joy of Sex* and other books. Then on Wednesday he spent time reading and looking at the pictures in the *Kama Sutra*. Then on the way home he stopped at the Sex Pantry, just to see what they had and to ask one of the girl attendants how each item was used. The girl showed him the latest tools and explained in a dry matter-of-fact way how they were used. He thought that all of this was important, and it added to his knowledge of how to love and please his wife. Those grey eyes of Angela's sparkled with more luster every day. Their marriage and love, which was always good, improved. He looked forward to coming home and finding her already there and relaxed.

In a way Angela was a neat freak. She cleaned up and discarded stuff no longer needed. From time to time, she gathered up stuff to throw away. He'd have discarded stuff, but he didn't want to throw away something she planned to keep. One day she was collecting back issues of newspapers and magazines, tying them together, and putting them in the recycle can.

She left for work before him, so he went out to look at what she'd discarded. The fashion magazines were there. All the worked crossword puzzles they'd done that past winter. Magazines advertising computer memory upgrades. Old discarded books of Sudoku, where she'd tried to teach him how to do the puzzles. Back issues of *Oprah* and *Atlantic Monthly* and *The New Yorker*. He finally came to the stuff from the garage. Yes, the tool magazines were there. He searched through them until he saw *10,000 Tools — A Tool for Every Job*. He flipped through it to the order blank that is usually inserted between pages. It was still there. He knew she never ordered by phone or from eBay or Craigslist.

He felt better knowing she'd thrown that magazine away. But he couldn't relax. He had to keep ahead of the jobs that turned up in the house. That garage door opener was sticking. He had to do something about that this evening. And he probably should tell her sometime that she is both pretty and smart, because you never knew when a copy of that tool magazine might show up again in the mail. Or maybe Angela would borrow one if she felt the need.

She was smart and up-to-date on everything.

CALLIE

IT WAS ABOUT SIX O'CLOCK on Sunday morning when I answered the phone. It was my little brother Shaun on his paper route.

"Is that you, Callie?"

He sounded scared, or shocked, or something; you know, not his usual brash, obnoxious self.

"Is that you, Callie? Is it you? I got to know who I'm talking to. There's somebody dead over here on my paper route."

"Dead?" I said, hardly believing what I was hearing.

"Yeah, a dead girl, lying all sprawled out under a tree near the sidewalk. She's naked. No clothes. Nothing! I think you know her."

"Me? I know her? Dead? Where? Where are you, Ben?"

"I'm on my paper route, over here a block from Marcy's AM/PM. It's on my route," he said. "You'd better tell Dad or Mom or somebody. I got to call the police."

I said. "Just wait a sec. Dead did you say? How do you know I know her? "

"I saw you with her one day after school."

"It's somebody from school then?"

"She was at the school a lot."

"Okay. Okay," I said. "Don't do anything. Just stay there. I'm coming over there. Is anyone with you?"

"No, the clock here at the store says 6:15. There's never anybody out this time on Sunday morning, I was just throwing papers when…" He paused.

"Just wait there. I'll be there in less than five minutes."

I threw on jeans and a t-shirt over my night things and ran out of the house. In about two minutes I found him outside the AM/PM. He didn't look so good. His eyes were all wild, darting about here and there. And he was biting his bottom lip. I could see he was scared, but he acted all important.

"I found her on my route," he said, as if he was telling it to his friends. He looked around as if he didn't quite believe it. "Wait. Wait until I tell Shaun and those guys. On my route. I asked Shaun last night to do the route with me, and he said he had to get his sleep. Just wait until he hears."

I said, "Okay, come on and show me the body. Where is it?"

He pointed down the street. "About two blocks. Hadn't we better call the police? Did you tell Dad?"

"No, I want to see her first. Who is it, do you know?"

"I don't know who she is, but she's around the school a lot. I saw you with her one day. I think she's your friend or something."

"Don't be saying she's my friend."

"She may be, 'cause I saw you two one day after school, talking with your faces close to each other."

We ran down the street, and I drew up sharply when we came to this big mottled birch with its soft swaying branches, with leaves moving almost tenderly caressing the body, this dead white body of a girl. Dead, lying on her back with everything, all of her private parts out showing. Her eyes were open, and the dew of morning was like tears in them. Her face was all quiet and serene, not like the Yvonne that we all knew, so passionate and caring and determined. Always telling. Just telling you something for your own good.

Now she was silent, her lips open with morning dew twinkling on a tooth, her lips kind of primped as though she was about to tell me something. And I seemed to hear better now the thing she'd been telling us.

But naturally my eyes ran over her breasts, down to her naked lower body with all of her private parts, brown tufts of hair showing. She was not my special friend, but I knew her. Yes, I had talked to her…or she'd talked to all of us about her experiences and told us we didn't want to go there. She was not my friend, but if I had listened, she might have been. Now I didn't want anyone to pass and see her like that. Even her legs were open. She didn't have on anything, panties or nothing. Not even shoes.

"Yvonne," I whispered her name. I didn't mean to say it.

And Ben said, "You do know her, then. Who is she?"

"She…She's Yvonne, a girl who used to go to school with us. She was older, and she dropped out a long time ago."

"If she was your friend, what are you going to do about it?"

"Why do you keep saying she's my friend? What can I do about it? Do? Do about what?"

"She's dead! If it were Shaun or those guys, you know, friends of mine. I'd do…some…thing."

"I plan to take care of myself, Ben," I said more quietly, "Go back to the AM/PM and call 911. Tell the police how you are a paperboy who found a body. Tell them where it is, and that you'll wait there for them. Don't answer any other questions. Just say you'll wait there for them. Tell them you've got to call your parents." After a little thought, I said, "Then call Mom and Dad and tell them what you found, and say I'm with you and we are watching the body until the police come."

Ben threw off his newspaper bag and ran to make the phone calls. I looked up and down the street. It was an early spring morning, and in the east the sky was all yellow and red. Everything was quiet, not a soul in sight. In the distance I heard traffic droning away on the freeway below. A bird or two flew by and perched in nearby trees. The air was cool. A slow breeze activated the birch branches as they almost swept the ground where Yvonne lay on the lawn near the sidewalk by a high fence.

The early morning air made me shiver thinking about her, lying there on the cold, damp grass. I was chilled and put my arms up around my shoulders. I looked up at the windows of nearby houses. They were shuttered like closed eyes. Across the street were an alley and the backs of several houses with cars parked on the street and in the alleyway. I looked back at Yvonne. And I looked closely at her arms and legs. They were pocked with healed white pricks marks. I tried to remember all I knew about her. She tried to help kids stay away from drugs.

Yvonne was always trying to get kids to stop using drugs. She'd done all types, and in a school assembly program she came and told the kids they were just destroying themselves. She didn't do them anymore, and she was trying to save us. Sometimes when she walked with us and talked to us, there were men and women in cars watching us. Once when we passed a car, a man rolled down the window, glared at us, and said to Yvonne, "What the fuck are you doing now?" And another time, the same person said, "Stop this shit you're doing. Don't mess with my business."

Yvonne glanced at them and behind our backs, as we walked along, I saw her give them the finger, and she said over her shoulder, "Screw you. You're the same guys that fucked up my life."

How did she get here? Was she an overdose? She didn't do drugs. I knew that. The body was too peaceful. I wish I knew more. She was the first dead person I had ever seen. I didn't feel comfortable standing there with her. It was hard to stay there by myself. I thought there could be people watching me. I thought of breaking some of the branches to cover her, but I remembered from television that you are not supposed to touch anything, so I just stared, and breathed heavily, and walked a short distance away from her. But I kept coming back to stare.

In about five minutes, a patrol car passed down along the street toward the AM/PM slowly and came back and parked across the street from where I stood with the body of Yvonne. The officer in the car glanced over to where I stood. He got on the phone and talked for a while. He didn't bother to get out or come near the body. He didn't say a word to me.

Ben came back and picked up his bag with the Sunday papers and said he had to finish his route. I told him he should wait a few minutes and tell the policeman how he found the body.

In another few minutes, people came from their houses and collected outside their doors. More police cars drove up. The officers chatted with each other. A few came over to where Yvonne lay, and a woman brought a crummy-looking stained blanket and asked a policeman, "in the name of decency," could she cover the girl's body? When she was permitted to do that, I looked with more concentration at the girl's arms and saw the old healed track marks up and down them.

Pretty soon after that I couldn't see much of anything because news photographers moved about snapping pictures, and one of those mechanical buckets that hold workmen went hovering over her with a photographer taking the coroner's pictures from every angle. About a dozen police officers loitered near the coroner, who looked and felt over Yvonne. It was obscene. I wouldn't want anyone putting their hands down there, swabbing up and down with Q-tips, even if I were dead. The cops stood around her, smoking cigarettes, and telling vulgar jokes. I heard one punch line: "I nearly lost my cookies." A police officer with a bullhorn warned us to stand back and to go about our business.

Ben went to do his paper route. I left after they'd taken her up on a stretcher into an ambulance car and were driving her to the morgue. I went off by myself and looked up at the sky and, through hot tears, said, "Why? She was good and tried to help me. I am the bad one, and she's dead instead of me. Why God? Can you tell me why?"

I walked around by myself for a long time, thinking about Yvonne and what she'd tried to do.

When the police left, I went back to see where she'd lain. The outlined print of her body showed where the pressure of her weight had pressed the grass down, but the footprints were erased. Where her legs had been, the grass blades stood almost straight. In a short time, all the grass would stand tall again, like she'd never been lying there at all.

The next day I anxiously grabbed a newspaper from Ben's delivery bag. I wanted to see what they wrote about her. I searched the paper, on every page, thinking with all the photographers and policemen recording things about the body, there'd be big news spread about how it happened and who did it. But there was no mention of Yvonne that day nor the next. They ignored her death entirely. I am still angry about that.

Sometimes when I think about Yvonne, I get very angry. When I see those men hanging around the school, talking to little kids, I want to chase the kids back into their classes. That's what Yvonne used to do. At times like those, I hear Ben's voice saying, "If she were my friend, I'd do something." It's funny, I never thought of her as a friend, but I guess she was.

GABRIEL

EVERY SUMMER WHEN SCHOOL IS OUT, I go to make money in the fishing fleets in Alaska. It's nice out there with nothing but the waves and the floating ice and men manning the nets and pulling in all kinds of fish. Except there are rules. Sometimes we have to throw back something interesting, because there are laws against you keeping them. What would you do with it anyway, that far away from Seattle?

If I work steady for two and a half months, I have my pockets full. I can send money to my family in Mexico and still have enough to pay for my apartment in Seattle with a little part time work in a restaurant I know during the winter. But this year is different. I won't make anything. I wish I'd gone on the crab boats. At least they aren't directly bothered by the oil spill. All that beautiful sky is there, but the water is covered with oil, the sky is without birds. People don't think about the little things until something happens that changes what they like in life. I used to think about it.

You see when men work alone, there is no need of people bringing their private life to the boat. A lot of men, I'd learned this, came to the boat to find young guys. But I say straight off, don't touch me or you're dead meat. I am not afraid of dying, and I say if someone bothers me, I am willing to die to keep them off me. That is not me, see. I love my girlfriend. She has our baby, and it is going to be our life, but I don't love no man that way. I told them loud and clear the first day, when they were talking and kidding around and trying to touch me when we were drawing in the nets and bending over it. It was the only unhappy part of the summer, where we slept and how some of the older men tried to treat some young boys who did not think like them.

I say boys because we were a good deal younger and came to the boats thinking of women and not interested in having sex with men. People who do that, I don't care. It is not my business. Just leave me out of it, and out there we had nobody to run to. We had to be strong fighters when someone constantly came after you, shoving you along the nets and into the tanks with the fish, jostling you when you were opening bulkheads or laying traps for you in your sleep. It was like a small ghetto, but not really, because in the ghetto you know where you are, and you don't take that fucking shit off nobody. But on the boat, it is do or die, and I woke up fighting when I recognized an intent to do that to me. After my knife blade slashed one guy along the side of his head from ear to below the chin, nobody else bothered me. They jeered at the cut guy. "Gabriel blew a trumpet in his ear."

But that's what I say. We young people are like a natural resource, and you got to look after us like the shoreline of the country where the water laps the land, the fish and birds are wild and free and fresh, and the air goes inside of you and lifts you out of the boat. In the morning, all you can think are big thoughts about life and what you want your life to be and your child's life, and you see the wide spread wings of the eagle flying overhead and you feel like that—soaring—and you hear the songs of the beautiful birds all around, flying in patterns, turning, and careening free. They wake you in the morning, calling to each other and feeding and sharing along the shore. And you see the flocks fly up from the water somewhere inland, and it is just like your heart moves up in your throat. If you know any song, you catch yourself just humming.

That was before the Exxon Valdez Spill, and it makes you know, if you don't take care of this, it is like a young person's innocence. It can be destroyed in one moment, a single night. But when a shock comes like that, no matter how great or small, we become less important, less great. I guess that sounds like crap to some, but I talked to this scientist once when they were building the pipeline, and he explained it all to me. That they had to work to get those tankers off the ocean, because they ruined everything. Then soon after I saw him and he said, "Now, Gabriel, you can see what I was telling you." Because then there was the spill, and it had ruined my job, and I had to do something else instead of working on the water and waves and ice and fresh air. I had to see for miles and miles oil drifting and covering the wonderful water, and the birds and fish and seals dead. All dead. Everywhere along the shore. And they couldn't show how bad it was on TV. Television just couldn't show how widespread it was. I kept wondering why couldn't they show it all, day after day, just how bad it was. I kept wondering, hey man, why can't they get it all, show what the Exxon Valdez did to everything. But that's why they got people reading, but it seems different when a few words can be substituted for something that big and devastating.

I couldn't earn any money fishing that summer, so I called Celia, my baby's mama, and I said. "Celia, it's a mess up here. Did you see on TV where a big oil tanker split and dumped all that oil?"

She said, "Yes, I saw it on all the time, but they don't show much. What you gon' do?"

And I said, "I don't know. The boats aren't going no place."

She said, "Why don't you come on back? I'm working, you know, and we can do all right."

She worked at the Round Table. I don't like to take nothing from her. I like to give to her, so I said, "Naw, you know what you make is not enough. I been talking to people, and I'm going to clean birds."

She started laughing right on the phone. "Clean birds? What are you saying, man?" I laughed with her, because I hadn't thought about it before I said it. Men don't usually clean babies where I come from, and now I was going to clean birds. It was really funny if you let your mind play with it. "Clean birds? What part of them?"

After we stopped laughing, I told her, "There are thousands of seals, fish, and birds dead and floating in the water, but there are many birds with oily wings and beaks that can be saved. The government is hiring people to clean off the oil."

She just listened and didn't say much. I said, "They're collecting these sick birds with oily wings and beaks, so oily they can't open them to feed. That's all the work they got up here, and I am taking a job tomorrow."

And then we talked about little Gabe and what he was doing.

"Just playing? Right?"

"Right here on the apartment floor."

And I talked to him a thousand miles away, and he knew his dad.

I told Celia about the two young Philippine fishermen they found floating in the gulf, their bodies all oily and their hands tied with cat gut. They'd been shot in the head, but they were floating like the birds and fish in the oily water. There is talk about rival fishermen and the union, and there is some kind of federal case. These kids were in the union and knew too much. They were sent from the Philippines. But you know, they are too young and innocent, with bullets in their heads and their black hair plastered to their heads with oil and their clothes soaked in oil. I went to see them when they brought them in. I had to see them.

She said, "Gabe, don't you get to know too much and get mixed up with it. I can't raise little Gabe without you. I mean, I'd never want to."

When she said that, I suddenly couldn't talk about it any longer. I went to bed, because I had to go for my job the next day with the bird and fish rescue teams. I couldn't help thinking of those guys all night. They had their own boat and fish station.

So I did bird cleaning. They had some really neat and sensitive people working on that project. They brought in these oily egrets and merlots and then these beautiful songbirds. Their feathers were oily pasted to their bodies, and their beaks were glued closed. I never knew how important a bird's arms are in balance when they walk. These birds were unbalanced, and if you cleaned one side and did not do an equal cleaning job on the other side where the wings could be lifted and lowered for balance, the birds would stumble and topple over.

I told Celia about Feral, that boy who goes to school with us. "He's here. I swear he's nuts or something. He almost cried one day when we came upon a lot of birds all lumped together. You couldn't tell anything. It was just a huge pile of feathers. It was shocking and pitiful, Celia. Feral was almost crying. He went off by himself and just stared up at the sky as if he was looking for a lost flock of birds."

Feral had said, "Gabriel, somebody is going to pay for this. And that somebody is us."

I didn't see how we could pay anything. We were just kids, going to school or trying to work on fishing boats.

But he said, "Gabriel, it's us, we're the ones who'll pay for this."

I really think he's crazy or something.

These birds couldn't open their beaks without help, and their air tubes and nacres are on the top of the beaks. That's how they breathe. I wish our biology teacher had been there. I could've got him to give me a biology grade for all I learned the short time I was there. But it was a lost cause. They died faster than we could save them. It was sickening. I couldn't take it. It paid good, but I left after two weeks.

I quit and went back to Seattle to take little Gabe to the parks and to hang out and kick it with Celia. I got a part time job in the Central District. I don't know what will happen, but I have only one year before I graduate.

BRIE

I DON'T KNOW HOW I GOT to the Mental Health Intensive Inpatient Detox Unit. I know after they took my car and sent me to that school, I didn't care what I did. I did Oxycodone, 'shrooms, Ecstasy, cocaine, meth, and I always did my stuff of choice. I did a lot of marijuana.

I do remember something of that morning in the principal's office. I must have still had a lot of the drugs in my system. After I went to Portland that weekend and did non-stop everything at that rave, I didn't know if my ass was up or down. Everything we took at that all-weekend day-and-night dance was laced with something. But who gave a good goddamn? I was the best looking and the best goddamn dancer there.

Mother let me go to Portland to stay with my cousin, but my aunt, my cousin's mom, was in Coos Bay, and we did what we wanted. And that was every fucking thing that came. We didn't know the fucking word No.

I didn't want to come to this damn school anyway. I had always gone to the best schools. I didn't relate to most of the kids here, and the teachers sucked big time. Both my parents are executives, and we have money to burn. We can live anywhere we want to. Every time one of them is promoted in their jobs, we move and the other one puts in for a transfer to the town where the other one was promoted.

We have been to Ohio, Michigan, California, and now Washington. I know my way around schools. Why can't I go to school anywhere I want to? I like Bellevue and Redmond.

Everything was cool. Until I made that one mistake and got caught with that pipe in my purse and sent to see the school counselor. How did I know they'd search my car? When they found all that shit—the marijuana and cocaine and mushrooms—they suspended my license, and my parents went damn ballistic, irate. The crap didn't even belong to me; someone left the shit in my car. My parents didn't like the three-month suspension and shifted me to this alternative school.

Today my parents are here in the school with me for a conference. It's about my attendance and my grades. They won't find a damn thing. They don't have the patience. They'll ask a few questions, and then they'll hurry to their damn Ivy League jobs. I've got the shit covered. Ever hear of Stone Wall? That's me.

Hey do you believe all that crap they say about addiction? I had this counselor at Terrace Academy. You know what he said? He said if you start doing chronic when you're very young, it affects the brain and you can't think properly. That's all a crock, because I had my first joint when I was eight and been smoking it ever since, and I think damn well. That's one lie they can forget.

It's the first time my parents have been to my school in two years. They have seen what I brought home, both grades and a report card. They are both busy intelligent professionals, and they trained me to take care of my business the way they take care of theirs.

I see they are calling me in now. The assistant principal is already with my mom and dad. He glanced at me when I came in and said, "Here's Brie's attendance record," handing a folder to my mom.

I breathed in and bit my top lip while watching my mother's face change as she looked at the paper. She looked at the assistant principal as if he was a moron.

"Obviously," she used her very tolerant, patient voice, "there's some mistake. This is not Brie's record. Since she had that trouble at the other school, I've taken care to deliver her here every morning myself."

My dad didn't say anything; he was busy looking at the student policy notices posted on the office wall.

My mother put the attendance report on the principal's desk, pulled a card from her purse, and put it beside the report on the desk. "You see here? These dates don't match. The report card is marked with perfect attendance, except in October. She was out with a cold. Then in November, she had that physical examination. All the rest of the time she was at school. So, how could this attendance record be accurate? No! Your records are mixed up."

She showed it to my dad. "Look here, Alex. I know this can't be accurate, because I dropped Brie outside of the school, right here on Broadway, every morning on my way to work."

The principal spoke on the phone to his secretary, asking her to bring teachers' reports of Brie's absences. "And have the counselor come in."

The counselor was this smiley, bookish type who wore classy blonde-tipped pointed glasses. Her lips crimpled at the corners of her mouth, looking as though she loved everybody, but then you could see the executioner's noose behind the smile that could change to smirky hate in a millisecond.

She saw me and said, "Hi, Brie. You're here?" It was more like a question than a greeting.

I nodded yes, but there was a big fat lump in my throat. The secretary came in and handed the principal a folded computer-generated sheet of paper.

The principal opened it and said, "Brie, you've been absent from math class seventeen days. In government, you've been absent fifteen days. That is an afternoon class. Either you left early or came to school late. I think you know the answer." He was about to read further, but he asked Mom, "Does that correspond with the days you dropped her off at school?"

Mom's mouth had flown open. She looked with consternation at Dad, shaking her head, and then glaring at me.

The counselor looked puzzled, and the paint-on smile disappeared. She sat in one of those swivel-around chairs, and she slowly turned her chair toward me. "Your mother dropped you at school? Brie, what about the bike?"

My dad became alert, looking arrows across the room at me. "What bike?" His eyeglasses were no longer fogged. The light from the window behind him danced and glared in them as he whipped his head around toward me.

"Yeah, bike?" I said. Trying to delay and confuse them.

"You kids call motorcycles bikes," said the counselor. "I mean the one I saw you and the boy arrive on or passed by on every morning. Or were you leaving? Remember, I waved at you several times through my office window."

In my mind's eye, I saw her raise the window and wave at me. I had just hopped on the bike after Mom dropped me off. The counselor saw the change on my face that indicated that I had made the connection. She nodded and the smile returned.

It was hot in here now. My face burned. I looked across the table at them all adults looking straight at me, wanting answers.

The room was too closed in. They were all too close. There was not enough air in the room. My mother's stare was like a cigarette lighter's flare. The heat and fire coming too close to my face. And I saw a haze of smoke rising from a bung. I couldn't breathe… and…And when I did… The air was…hot. Then I was the bung, hot and being burned, and the stuff was coming up in my nose. I didn't give a shit about anything.

I yelled, "It's not even half as important as you guys think it is. I don't have a problem. You guys have hella problems. All of you guys are tripping. Why can't you let us the hell alone? You have lived your crummy, damn, useless lives. Now you want to live ours. It's always success and the office and getting ahead. It's a damn race to fucking nowhere. Get off me! Get off my fucking back! Back off! Leave me the fuck alone."

I was flinging books and stuff and pushing over chairs. In my mind it was like I was jumping on or off a motorcycle, and I was getting the hell out of there.

I don't know what happened after that in the principal's office. I know Mom was holding me, and she was shivering or shaking and calling out in a weak voice for Dad. "Alex. Alex." Mom was holding me, and Dad was saying to me, "Stop it! Now, just stop it!" I thought he was going to slap me, but he didn't. He just brought me to him and rubbed my back. I was out of control. Crying, screaming.

But nobody could make me stop it. I was high there and didn't give a damn. I was back in Portland at the rave and I…I…they told me I danced in the principal's office.

Then I woke up in the Mental Health Unit. With Mom and Dad and everyone standing over my bed. Looking at me with worried faces.

All I could think was, "What the hell happened?"

LAYTRICE

I AM A GOOD STUDENT, a basketball player, and a track star. I can do anything in sports that anybody else can do. Colleges are all after me. I mean they are on the phone with my mother night and day. The U wants me. State wants me to play for them. Mother says, "Remember, Laytrice. Keep your head up, girl. Keep on doing what you doing."

I told her, "Mama, my grades are good. Boys and stuff are on the back burner. I don't have time for that right now."

That's what it was like. No boy could tell me anything I wanted to hear. But now I know that no matter how strong you think you are, things can slip up on you. It's bad to get wrapped up in things, because that's when you stop watching and you think you're all right. I never listened to any boy until Delroy came slowly creeping up on me. That's what it was. Delroy sneaked up and stole my future.

It started out like a fun day. I was kicking it down at Seward Park with him, my boyfriend, Delroy Saunders. He is a little older, had finished school, and was out working and bought this new car. It was a Stinger, shiny with all this chrome and big lights and a radio, and he'd put on this cool, deep sound. I mean you could hear us coming a block away. And the resonations of the music blasted in your chest and head, and people would be looking around. It was impossible to ignore us.

The drive at Seward Park is circular, and we go up, winding around among the trees and flowers. I had let him drive me there after practice two or three times, and it was relaxing after running laps to just lay back in the car under the big rhododendron bushes with the pink and purple flowers hanging across the road, almost into the car, and the cool breeze of the lake just touching and caressing your whole self.

We parked way up, on the circular level on the side where we could look out of one side and see the lake, the water, the boats, and people walking along concrete walks along the lake below us. But there was shrubbery all around us and nobody could see us. It was like Delroy's tinted windows; we could see out okay, but nobody could see inside the car.

It was the first time I really let him kiss me. Delroy had his big old hands all over me where they had no business being, and I was just laughing at the fool because he was funny and tried to do and say things that got me tickled. Like saying, "Laytrice, I bet I can make you cum without us putting it in or anything."

That in itself should have sent up a danger sign, because before this, when I heard things like that, I'd open a car door, jump out. Slam it! And I'd be long gone.

But I listened to the smooth fool. He followed that up by sticking his hand under my blouse, catching the tip of my nipple, and rubbing it gently through his thumb and forefinger, making me crazy and setting me to giggle more. I didn't listen to my true self. I was just slipping into and enjoying something new.

I tried to make myself angry and get up the nerve to leave there right then. But that moment slipped away. Then he slowly inched his right hand down inside my pants. His hand had discovered where my panties were, and his hand was inside there sliding by where my stomach and hip met to the spot where my legs joined in front. Then in the center, where I felt his fingers moving in the hair there, and I jumped. I think he was right in what he'd said, because I was quivering like a leaf in warm wind.

But I was concerned. It was early dusk, and cars could come and people could walk up on us doing what he was thinking, what we were thinking. I was thinking about AIDS and condoms and pregnancy. All these came and sat on the dashboard in front of me. And still I didn't do anything. I was stupid. Just plain stupid! I knew from experience if Delroy got to a certain point, it'd be very hard to delay him, to stop him. I tried to slow down the kissing. I joked with him and guided his hands back toward the steering wheel, and I was trying to get his mind slowly on to something else. That wasn't working, and we were scrunched down in the seat, almost ready to go after it.

But out of the tail of my eye, I saw this car coasting around the curve, light flashing on its windows, passing us slowly. I jumped up trying to see if I recognized anyone in it. I couldn't see who was inside, but they drove so slowly, they almost stopped beside our car—like they recognized it. Then they moved off quickly. I thought something was wrong. Then I knew it when Delroy, moving slowly. He reached under his seat and brought out this big-assed hand gun that I never knew he had. The car took off. You know how the road goes around. We were relieved, because everything there is one way. They couldn't back up or turn around there.

Delroy got out and went behind the big rhododendron to pee. While he was gone, they must have driven down hurriedly, because the car came zooming back fast, the tires crying and whining on the tarmac. It stopped just for a quick second by our car, and that was when its tinted window whizzed down. I quickly scrunched lower in my seat, but the bullets came so fast and so many that it sounded like one loud long gun blast, with metal zinging and bullets screeching and crying off it, and smoke and this stinky smell. I felt jabs in parts of my body, but right then it didn't hurt. There was blood, but it didn't hurt. And I heard the tires of their car whining on the concrete. Just like that, they were gone.

I couldn't hear anything, and it seemed like the world stopped.

Then Delroy was yelling, "Oh, damn…Look at this!"

I don't know how much of the rest of this because I saw it, and how much Delroy told me later. But he saw the shattered windows, with glass everywhere, and saw I was shot bad with blood all over the seat and all over me. He said over and over, "Laytrice! Laytrice! Oh, my God, Laytrice. I am so sorry. Those goddamn sons a'bitching fools." He touched me and tried to hold me for a minute, but he was scared and kept on repeating, "You hurt badly, Laytrice. You sure is hurt bad, Laytrice. I got to get you to the hospital." And he drove like he was crazy, curving back down the hill to the street, hitting bushes, going through red lights, and cutting in front of cars, dodging in and out of traffic on the way to Harborview.

But I didn't know anything because I passed out. I woke up in the middle of the night. They'd already done two or three operations on me. I was drugged and didn't feel much of anything. I thought that was the reason I couldn't feel anything in my legs or hips or arms. Everything else was all right.

But I am a track star, for Jesus's sake. I can out run any girl in the high schools of Seattle. I play basketball. I am the best, eighteen points a game. I am the star, and now I can't feel anything in my arms and legs. I can't do anything for myself. I am here in the hospital, and people have to turn me over because I can't do it for myself. They have to lift me up, feed me, and take me to the bathroom. I can't even go to the bathroom by myself. I am a woman, eighteen years old, and I am a vegetable. I can't do anything for myself. What kind of a life is this?

Delroy comes to see me. It's been two months now. I passed a birthday in here. I ask him what the police found out about it. He just looks away. He has something I didn't know about. Before he finished school and got his present job, he used to sell crack cocaine. My mother came with red sore eyes and told me everything. He quit and made somebody angry, because he knows their business and didn't want to sell anymore. His mother begged him to quit. He quit. And he wouldn't cooperate with his homies any more.

But I keep wondering about that big gun that he pulled from under his seat, and I wonder why at that particular time he went out to pee. It's like he knew they were after him. He still looks around suspiciously while he's visiting me here in the hospital. I keep thinking why he didn't shoot into their car. But they were his homies, so he couldn't kill them.

I am the one they got. I am an innocent person who knew nothing.

I sometimes wish they, whoever they are, would find him here in the hospital and finish the job. Kill both of us, together. I wouldn't mind. He said the police tried to get him to tell. "Rat," he called it. They wanted to know who on Mercer Island and in Bellevue he used to sell to and buy from. He wouldn't tell because he didn't want to rat and didn't want to deal anymore. He was lucky he wasn't hit, but look at me. What good am I to myself? He comes to see me and says he loves me, but what is that and how long will his words last? What's my future? What can I do? I know I don't deserve this, but young people got to start watching and listening and finding out who to trust and everything about people they are with, because they don't know what can happen.

When I go back to school, I have to go in a wheelchair. Right now, I don't know if I want to do that. What's the use of going to school when an innocent person can be cut down without warning? I still let Delroy come around to see me, but to tell the truth, I really don't want him around anymore. I blame him, you can believe that. It was all his fault.

MUGGED

Imagination is "the Saviour" that releases humanity
from the prison of experience.
—Blake

STRANGE THINGS HAPPEN TO YOU sometimes when you're alone. You have no one who witnesses them, and later when you discuss what happened, no one can believe it actually did. That's the way it was with Travis Perkins. He spent time alone. His wife worked during the day and nights she either went to church or to a women's club meeting.

She was a good wife! Travis loved her, but she had two habits Travis couldn't stand. She complained about his active imagination and drank coffee constantly from the same cup. That cup followed her from room to room, and as she moved about, she made periodic trips with it to the kitchen. When she put up curtains, made beds, played the piano, or even weeded the garden, that cup was always near her hand. She held it, caressed it, her lips brushed it, and Travis thought that sometimes she talked to it. That cup was forever there, between them.

From the time Travis saw his wife with that cup, he could not stand the smell of coffee. The odor of caffeine gave him fits. His nose started a twitch he couldn't control. His eyes looked at her and quickly darted away. When she spoke to him, he didn't say much or didn't answer at all. He moved away quickly when she came near him while fondling that cup. He hated that coffee mug.

Angie knew Travis had all kinds of "fixations" about her coffee mug. She'd been through it all with him before. She'd even changed coffee mugs several times before because of it. Now they were fairly comfortable, she thought, most of the time with this one. Only rarely did Travis revert to his child-like behavior: upsetting his chair, knocking things over on the table at meals, or almost throwing a tantrum about the mug.

The thing with his imagination was comic, if you really thought about it. Angie once said playfully, "I believe you're jealous of Kaffee Mug." She gave the cup a playful name to tease him. But Travis did not laugh at the joke; he did not think it funny; he did not like the mug and hated that caffeine smell.

"It's not the caffeine so much as it is the way you think about it. Your imagination is what makes our love making so good," she said. "You let your imagination run away with you." She loved to tease him that way.

He waited until one night when she was away to carry out the plan to rid himself forever of his porcelain rival. As soon as she left the house, he went into the sewing room, where he'd last seen her working, to get the cup. But it wasn't there. He explored the bedroom with no luck. He searched atop the piano, then near the ironing board and went on to snoop among the washed cups in the pantry. He even rummaged the potting shed in the garden and the patio. But it was nowhere.

"It's hiding from me," he said.

He turned cagey and backtracked. He quickly entered her study where he thought for sure he'd searched before. "Ah, hah," he caught a glimpse of the caffeine lips, scrunched down behind several books and a sheaf of papers, peering out at him from beside the computer mouse. Pretending his attention was drawn in another direction, Travis sneakily removed the book to disclose the hiding place and rapidly caught the mug in a firm grasp before it could glide away.

He put his hand into the single ear lobe and lifted its body from the table. It rested there in his hand with its wide mouth open, but not smiling or speaking, acting smug and confident that Travis wouldn't let it fall.

But it was about to learn a lesson, because Travis frowned as the odor from its mouth wafted up to him. He scrunched up his nose so he wouldn't get the full scent of its breath.

"Un huh, strong coffee and it's not even decaffeinated... uh... ach... agig...gah...stinky caffeine." These were all garbled sounds from Travis's mouth. "Okay, then you get washed." Or, he smiled. "You get broken," he said, shaking it loosely by the handle. This talk and quick motion upset the cup, which puked half of its contents on the floor. Some of the warm liquid splashed onto Travis's pants leg. The acrid sourness assailed Travis's nose. "It has coffee grounds in it, too. This cup is sick."

Worse still, Travis swore he heard a belch accompanying the breath that swept out of the mug's mouth. Travis made a motion as if to dash the cup toward the kitchen trash bin. The quick motion brought his shoe in contact with the slippery liquid on the floor. He skidded in it, one foot left the floor, to be quickly followed by the other, and Travis's whole body followed, flipping then landing with his back hitting the floor, giving off a cracking sound.

At first Travis was stunned; then he realized he was seriously hurt and couldn't move. He also felt the coffee mug on top of him, resting on his chest with its mouth open under Travis's nose. "It is as though that stupid cup threw me and is lying on me to hold me down," Travis thought. His nose twitched, irritated by the cup breathing caffeine right into his nostrils and…there was nothing he could do about it. Absolutely nothing. He tried again to move, first an arm…Nothing! He tried to move a leg… again, no response. Each time, he felt helpless and ready to panic; his head ached, and he wanted to puke. He willed himself to move, to get up. There was not even a twitch anywhere.

"I've got to do something."

Sweat poured from his face, around his ear. The sound of his voice brought some calmness. Maybe his stomach and chest muscles could work. He'd flex them and throw the coffee mug off his chest. He breathed deeply and tried to flex, but couldn't sustain it. The panic slowly returned. He couldn't think clearly.

"Get up! Lie quietly! Why hurry? Nothing is wrong! My back is broken! I could die here!"

All these thoughts raced through his mind at the same time.

He bit down on his bottom lip several times. What a pleasure to feel the result of some motion. He felt sensation about his face and mouth. His cheeks and mouth were working.

"At least I can turn my head. Why didn't I think of this before? If I move my head a little to the side, the cup will roll off."

He moved his head.

He rolled his head to the side.

The cup rolled with it.

When his head stopped its sidewise turn, the cup rolled until his shoulder stopped it under Travis's nose. He fiercely rolled his head in the opposite direction. The cup again rolled with the moving head. Either way he rolled, the cup landed under his nose. Travis tried not breathing, but eventually he had to breathe. How dangerous this cup was. He could just lie here and wait for Angie to come home and rescue him from this mug. He tried to stay awake but then he found himself all warm and relaxed on the floor. The caffeine scent had faded. He guessed he'd spilled most of the coffee and he no longer felt hyper. He felt relaxed as he nodded off. But after a short time, he awoke with a jerk. He did not try to get up or anything. He lay there. He tried to talk to himself but couldn't.

The cup was cold against his cheek as if it were asleep.

"This cup is vicious, and I don't want anything to happen to Angie as it did to me. I have to warn her, tell her about the cup. But how? Somehow, I will have to warn her not to do anything, not to try to do anything to this cup, for it can tell. It is intelligent and in good physical shape. After all, it threw me down and paralyzed me, and now it's breathing in my nose."

Travis awoke to the sound of the door opening.

"Hello." It was Angie's usual greeting whenever she returned home. "Oh why, Travis, are you and Kaffee Mug lying so cozily cheek to cheek on the study floor? You both missed me?"

She was down on the floor, kissing Travis and lifting the mug off his chest. He didn't know how it all happened, but now that she was here, he vaguely remembered this had all happened before, and now she knew exactly what to do.

Angie held Travis's hand and said, "Come on, Travis, my sweet, get up now." She repeated it several times while laughing and kissing him. "Get up. Come on now, Travis. Get up, and let's go to the kitchen."

And Travis found he could actually move his body. With almost no effort, her hands, soft and gentle, coaxed him up. He moved slowly toward her, smiling and relieved. He followed her directions, and soon they were all in the kitchen. He watched her beautiful flowing movements as she began making supper while talking to her husband and drinking coffee from her favorite mug. She took a sip of coffee and turned to him in her smiling, joking manner.

In her usual teasing voice, she said, "Travis, honey, you are sweet and I do love you. But you have an overactive imagination, and sometimes you just let it take over, willy-nilly, and you simply overreact."

He sat staring at her, feeling all warm and content.

After a moment she came near. Looking directly at him, she said, "You know, Travis, that imagination has its place. After supper we'll find the best way to use it."

CLEMMY

I LAY ON THE BED AND I must've slept, because when I woke up, the first thing I noticed was I couldn't move my arms. Something heavy was pressing down on my back. At first, I didn't know what was happening. I tried to bring one arm around in front of me. I couldn't. I was lying on my stomach and my face was pressing into the sheet, cutting off my breathing. I coughed and tried to turn over. Something held my shoulders in a grip. I stopped for a minute and tried to think.

Then I remembered coming home.

I let myself in with my key, and nobody was there. I thought my mother would be at the door like a crossing guard telling me what to do. I hadn't been home in two days. The minute I went to my room, I saw she'd picked up my blouses and put everything away and the room was neat. I could almost hear her voice, "Clemmy, baby you are a young woman now, sixteen years old. You've got to care more about yourself and your things."

But she wasn't home.

And I was...tired. I just came to look for my beeper and cell phone. Where in hell were they? I couldn't understand their disappearing. I can't do business without them, but right now I was...yawn...sleepy...I'd just lie down on the bed for a few minutes, then I'd go and meet Baye in the Central District, but I needed that damn cell phone. I lay on the bed and I must've slept. Then I smelled my mother's scent, her perfume.

I said, "Mother, what do you think you're doing?"

I knew it was her. It had to be her. Something in my foggy memory told me it was like something she'd do.

"Just be quiet, baby," she said. "It's for your own good."

That's when I found she's spread across my back, pushing down with her full weight. She was heavy as hell and wrapping something around my legs. Whatever it was, it was damn tight. She kept on making it tight, pulling and squeezing and tying something in knots. I felt that. She's trying to tie me up. She hadn't done anything like this since I was a little girl, about four or five years old, and we used to play in the flower garden.

"Mom, you heard me, what the hell are you doing this time?"

I struggled with her, trying to turn my body over, but she was too heavy and I didn't have the use of my arms or legs. She already had some part of me tied up and now she was tying my legs. I kicked at her as feebly as I could, my legs flipping but not touching her. I found I was helpless.

"Whatever you're meaning to do, it won't work, and you know it won't. You can't control me."

I twisted my body and got part of one leg from under her. I tried to scare her with my yelling. But she just went on tying me up and talking calmly and reasonably the way she has always done.

"Just be quiet, Clemmy. It's your mother. You remember how I used to do this with you in the flower garden. You liked it then."

That was a long time ago. I was no baby now. I had things to do I had my own life. Nobody could steal me now. My mind flashed back to what she'd told me about those times. It was a time when young children disappeared. People stole them from stores and parks when parents weren't watching closely. Mom told me then you could be walking with your child in the park and if you looked away for just a moment or did not pay attention, the child might wander away to look at something. Someone grabbed the child, and you looked and looked, but your child was not there. Your child was gone. Many children were stolen that way, and parents never saw them again. Stolen and you never got the child back.

She nicknamed me after the clematis plant in which she used to wrap me with its flowers all around my head and face, the beautiful vines. She'd pick red, pink, and purple wild flowers and put them in my hair, saying, say, "My Clemmy. You look like a beautiful flower. Bad people don't want flowers, Clemmy." She'd stand me away from her to have a look, flowers in my hair and we'd both be smiling and she'd say, "People are stealing children like you. I have disguised you as a flower. You are a flower." She hugged me close and said, "Now nobody will ever steal you from me."

But now what the hell was she doing? She'd changed into one of the bad people trying to control me.

She kept on wrapping my legs with something. I turned my face, shocked to find it was a twisted pantyhose. She was tying me up with my pantyhose. Now I was really mad. I had to think of some way to get her off me. She can't stand to hear me use vulgar language, so I said, "Mom, why in hell are you doing this? Let me go, bitching whore. Take your god-damn hands off me." I went on. "I don't want a sluttish whore tying up my goddamn legs, see? Take your low life, dirty bitching hands off me."

I was loud and mean as hell. I felt her body slacken. She loosened her hold, but kept on talking. I kept up the yelling and threw out as many bitches and bastards as I could mix in and said, "What the fuck do you think you are up to?"

I knew that'd get her. She'd never heard me go there before. I was glad I didn't see her face. But she wheezed, crying like a kid, loosened her hold, and got off my back. She can't stand to hear me curse. She got off me. She cried and sneezed. I glanced up and saw the glazed eyes and heard the whimpering, her shoulders jerking. Her hands were now up to her face, and she was wiping at her eyes and face. I was busy kicking, getting my shoulders out, untying and untwisting the damn hose, while she was shaking her head. I said a few more bitches and hells so she wouldn't decide to come back. Then she went into the Church thing.

She said as if she was praying. "I don't believe it, God. I never knew my own baby would say such things to her own mother who is trying to save her life."

I was almost free of the tangle of three or four pairs of pantyhose. I said, "Take care of your own damn self. You go where you want to go. I can go where I want to go."

She'd come back to where I was wriggling free of her ties and loops and twists in the hose. She tried to look into my face. All the while I am struggling to untie the last pantyhose knots that she has twisted up and down my legs. The woman was serious, but I needed to be free to go. I had to be somewhere in a few.

She said, "You don't find me going off and staying away two or three days. Or staying out until three in the morning, doing drugs with those Baye drug gang bangers."

"Kevin. His name is Kevin, and he doesn't sell any drugs. And if he did, Mom, it'd be his own fucking business." I could see her wince when I said that, but I had to get her out of my face.

"You sell drugs and you take them. You're on dope, and so is that Kevin, Byit or Bayeit, or whatever is his name."

"You see, you don't even know who you're talking about." I was almost free of the last knot now.

"I do know him. Everybody knows him. He has cell phones and pagers. He uses them to take drug orders, and there is some kind of code you have to say. You must be helping him. How did you get those little plastic bags of marijuana that I found in that pop can under your bed?"

I stopped in the middle of removing the last pantyhose, then flung it off and yelled at her. "You're fucking out of your mind. You've been under my bed? Where is the goddamn pager? You are going to get me in trouble. What did you do with the goddamn pager?"

She didn't answer me. She just folded her arms and looked sadly at me. And I judged by her look that she hadn't found my other stuff. She hadn't searched the bathroom up behind the toilet where I'd taped the packet.

She left the room crying that next she'd hear I'm dead from an overdose of cocaine or heroin, crying how she'd lost her baby, her only child, and lord, what had she done wrong to deserve such a punishment.

I couldn't talk to her. I went to the bathroom. We used to be close, but now you couldn't talk to her. She has to remember or know that…she has to realize that people and times change. I am not a baby. I am a grown woman, sixteen years old. She's tripping.

I got dressed. I had to meet Baye in the Central District. She kept crying all the while I was getting ready to split. Then she pleaded as if it was a matter of life or death. Man, adults are a pain in the ass. They don't know when to shut the fuck up.

No, it's, "Don't go, Clemmy. Please don't go. I forgive you for everything you've done or said. Let's work it out. You can be different. This is not the real you. Just don't go tonight. You are mama's flower. I want to take care of you."

"I don't want to be different. I don't want you to take care of me."

She went on sniveling like a brat that needs his nose wiped. "You used to go everywhere with me. Remember? I was so proud of you. I'd never leave you home alone, and I used to take you to the office with me. Didn't you like that?"

I had to admit that I did like that. I loved all of that, but it was a long time ago. I had other plans and other things I liked now and with her it was all or nothing. Then fine, it would be nothing. You had to be careful or all this "love you" junk would wear you down

She came up in my face, trying to turn the clock back to that time, trying to be all motherly and tender the way she always was. I had to think for a minute or she'd have me thinking like a kid, so I used my usual escape—bad language. She can't stand to hear me curse. "Just leave me the fuck alone."

She backed off right away.

"I swear I don't know when that school is going to kick all of you out, or you could end up shot on the sidewalk like that girl in Ballard or like that big handsome football player Garth, the night after his best game. I know you remember him, a fine athlete. You ought to know. You were a majorette at that very game. I saw you jumping so proud. You were so beautiful. What's happened to you? What is happening to all of you? This is no game."

I snatched on my clothes, got the package from behind the toilet, and hauled ass out of there. When I walked out, she was crying like a pack of babies. Something about losing her Clemmy. Man, she was really tripping.

LORNA

LORNA KNEW SHE'D FOUND THE right bar, because Len's red truck with the right bent fender was parked out front. She stood outside for a few minutes, getting up the courage to do what she had to do. Among the passersby were several men who turned their heads, taking notice of her tanned face and well-shaped body in its high-cut blouse and blue skirt, slightly longer than the present style.

Lorna searched in her purse until she found a tiny booklet, opened it, and nodding her head, read three lines from it. When she closed the booklet, her blue eyes sparkled with new energy. She reached up with a determined pull, forcing several strands of wayward blonde hair back behind her ear.

She stepped from the sun-streaked street into the dimness of the bar, where her nostrils were assaulted by mingled odors of cigarette smoke, stale beer, and sawdust. She felt the cushiony unevenness of the sawdust beneath her feet as her eyes searched the room while she wove her way among the drinkers who talked loudly to each other.

Those near her raised a stein of beer toward their lips or watched the big-screen TV high above them, which just then presented an argument between the umpire and a player who'd been called out at home plate.

About a third of the drinkers in the bar were women. Although she tried not to judge anyone, the word *coarse* intruded upon her thoughts as she glanced at their clothing, the loose skirts and low v-cut blouses, and heard the loud, animated conversation.

The bartender's long arms shuttled drinks up and down the bar to customers who shouted competition for his attention. It seemed to Lorna that he could reach clear into booths that lined the opposite wall.

She searched until she saw Len and Billy sitting in a booth midway in the room, a pitcher of beer in the center of the table and a full mug in front of each of them. She paused at the booth, placing her hands on the damp table of the booth, peering at both men. She glanced from one to the other, giving each a warm smile.

"Hi," she said. "You both missed your supper."

The older man, dressed in an airline mechanic's uniform, rose up, glaring at Lorna. He slapped the table with an open palm, causing the pitcher and mugs to dance about on the table. "Lorna, what in hell..." he began.

The younger one, Billy, in the process of drinking, nearly spat back into his beer mug. "How did you know we were here?" He wiped his mouth with his sleeve.

"I walked until I saw the truck parked outside. The Lord wanted me to come."

The young man wagged his head derisively. "He told you that?"

"What? No. Okay, you can joke about religion. You're always like this when you drink." She turned to her husband. "Why don't you both come on home to supper?"

"What's there to eat?" said Billy.

Len shook his head and yelled in her direction, spraying out beer. "Whatever she's got, it's no damn good, even if people are always chasing after her."

"Look, Len, I'm your wife, and nobody's chasing after me. Not even you. I'm a good wife, Len. Think about that."

Their faces were near; hers soft and gentle; his threatening.

"You're a damn rotten cook. I'll vouch for that." He poked his face nearer, then jerked it back to pay attention to his drink. He slurped, half finishing the beer in his glass before he yelled, "And look, where in hell are the damn children?"

Lorna still held her smile. Her hand moved toward him in a soft welcoming gesture, palm up, and open toward him.

"The children are with Mary Ellen as usual, across the street from us."

"Then goddamn it, go and get them, and give 'em their supper. As you can see, we're drinking ours." Len laughed and slapped the table. His loud speech attracted other patrons, and a few loud guffaws chimed in from around the bar among the drinkers.

Lorna brought her face lovingly close to Len's. "I cooked you a nice supper. Won't you come on home now, and let's eat together and...talk."

"Where have you been? Where were you when I came home?" Len glared at her.

"Why, at the church pool. We agreed about that on Thursday. You know how I like to swim. I told you. I asked you to come down and get..."

"You've got to show yourself in those skimpy bathing suits. Can't be happy unless men are drooling over you."

"Hon, there were no men there. It's women's night," Lorna whispered. "Now, Len, please don't talk to me like that here. You're angry because I went swimming, then let's talk about it at home... These people," she whispered, glancing around. "Just... can we talk at home?"

Len took several big swallows from his beer glass and poured more from the pitcher. Billy, while watching his dad, did the same.

Lorna slid toward the end of the booth and gently touched Billy's arm. "Billy, why don't you get up and go on to the truck? I want to talk to your father."

"Billy, don't you go no goddamn where," Len said.

Lorna shrank against the wood of the booth, her eyes glazed over. She looked humbly at Len.

"Len, do you think that is the right thing to say?"

Len didn't answer, and Billy kept his seat.

Lorna said in a quiet mournful voice, "Len, I've stood a lot from you." Her voice was soft and gentle. "You've come home and, for no reason, you've shouted, cursed, and beaten me for no reason. If I cooked lasagna, you wanted roast beef. If I cooked ham, you wanted turkey. Nothing pleases you. So, you slam me around. But this is worse."

She caught Billy's arm and said in a soft, but firm voice, "Billy, I don't approve of you drinking, and you know it. Stop it, and go to the truck."

Billy reared his head toward his mother and said, "I don't believe in my mother showing her body like a common hooker."

Lorna's head snapped away from him as though she'd been struck a powerful blow. Her mouth quivered and her blue eyes overflowed. Her head rose slowly, and she looked long and lovingly at him as though he were a sick baby. She said softly, sadly, "Billy. Billy."

Her tanned face was red now, and she felt very hot. She was oblivious to the eyes staring at her from around the bar. The bar was silent.

She said, "Len, you see. You're turning the children against me. And I have never opposed you. You've got control. What are you afraid of?" She shook her head. "Sometimes I think our troubles go back farther than us. Maybe somewhere in the family's past." She sighed. "Maybe even to your father and mother who drank and—"

She abruptly stopped in mid-sentence, sensing she'd made a terrible mistake. Len's face changed in an instant. Deep lines appeared at the corners of his mouth, his eyes yellowish red. Her face took on an alarmed, frightened look. She snatched at her purse. It eluded her, falling to the floor. Lorna hurried then to stand, but she did not move fast enough.

With one fierce sweep, Len shot out his hand, moving in a wide arc across the table, sending the pitcher and mugs flying from the booth into the room, dashing them against the barstools, shattering shards of glass over the sawdust floor where they winked in the light like crushed ice.

Lorna dashed for the door, feeling the squishy, yielding sawdust underfoot. It slowed her progress. She pushed open the door, bursting out into the sunshine. Running. Crying. Mumbling to herself. "He is turning the children against me."

Inside the bar Billy picked up his mother's purse from where it had fallen on the floor. A small booklet fell to the sawdust. He retrieved it and read: *Personal Bible Verses to Live By*. He remembered then a passage read in his mother's church: *The form of the world is passing away*. He took his mother's purse back to the booth, but let the pamphlet slip from his hands back to the floor among the sawdust and broken glass.

ON THE PLAYGROUND

Stephanie Breaks is ten years old, tall and slender, and there's a tooth out in front of her mouth, with a small new one just showing through the gum. You see it when she smiles. I had heard about her, because her sister is in the sixth grade and has had problems throughout the school. Stephanie is in fourth grade and very good at tether ball, but her fame was established on the monkey bars. Everyone, it seemed, knew how dangerous it was to play with Stephanie on the monkey bars.

The first time I saw her was on a blustery day in March, when kites fluttered and strained in the wind above the houses where their tethers were anchored to chimneys or roofs. Alicia Van Driel and Stephanie ran up to me.

Alicia cried, "Mr. Hyton, Mark Diller threw Stephanie's coat on top of the portable."

Mark Diller was a new boy who didn't know his way around on the playground and was trying hard to be known. Alicia was blonde, blue eyed, and chubby, while Stephanie had brown hair, freckles, and the coolest gray eyes I'd ever seen.

She was calm when I asked her: "Where was your coat?"

"On the ground. We were playing four square when he took it, tried to skip rope with it, holding the arms out like this. Then he slung it by the arm to the top of the portable."

She pointed, and we could see the coat lodged up there, resembling a child with one arm dangling from the side of the building. The building was tall, and the coat was up too high for me to reach. A few of the biggest boys and girls tried to basketball-jump it down, but it was higher than the nets on a basketball hoop. I didn't find out until the janitor brought it down that the coat held a rock in one of its pockets.

Stephanie took the coat without comment. I told her to come with me. I found the red-headed Mark and stopped his fast-moving tennis-shoe movements in kickball long enough to explain to him that his act was impolite, and shouldn't he apologize? He smiled and tossed his red hair. When he thought my attention had been drawn away, he folded his right fist, leaving only the middle finger showing, and pointed it up in the air, jabbing it toward Stephanie. I acted as though I hadn't seen it.

"Apologize for throwing Stephanie's coat on top of the portable, Mark," I urged him.

But Alicia was outraged. "Oh, Mr. Hyton, didn't you see that? He gave Stephanie the Great Silver Bird."

Mark Diller said, "I didn't do nothing. I'm new."

"Are you going to apologize?"

He didn't answer. I stood there waiting. Soon he looked over to where the game of kickball had resumed without him. He looked back at me. I hadn't moved and the serious expression on my face must have served notice on Mark that this could go on for the whole recess. He kicked the tarmac, saying, "Sorry. Okay?" Then, giving me a sidewise glance, he stuck his tongue out at Stephanie.

Stephanie and Alicia returned to the sports they were both good in, which was everything! Alicia could do all sports, but Stephanie was a natural. She's exceptional at tumbling and any form of gymnastics. She gets highest points in PE, physical endurance, and skills tests. She does curl-ups until the PE teacher gets tired and says, "Okay, Stephanie." Stephanie goes from that to push-ups, then jumping jacks. "That'll be enough, okay? I said okay, Stephanie. Go on to the trampoline." Stephanie's face lights up at that. She tumbles off and on the trampoline with such ease, it's astounding for a child her age.

A few minutes after the coat incident, I saw her whipping the tether ball around the pole so fast that her opponent, Nancy Wade, a sixth grader, cried, "Gosh, Stephanie, you don't give anybody a chance."

That was a normal playground complaint, so I walked over to the basketball hoops to watch some kids trying to get the ball high enough to touch the nets. A few minutes later, near the swings, I saw a moving flash zoom down the big slide and strike Mark in the back. When I reached him, he was face down on the tarmac, crying. I lifted him up. His arms and face were raw where they'd scraped the hard playground surface from the force of his fall. He was bleeding.

"What happened?" I asked.

A group of children had collected around Mark. "Stephanie did it," they chorused. I instinctively looked toward the tether ball pole. There she was, pretending not to notice us, zooming the ball around the pole, laughing playfully with Alicia.

This incident was serious enough to get mothers in. They met in the principal's office. The principal later told me what happened.

"This child is dangerous," said Mrs. Diller, pointing at Stephanie.

Stephanie 's mother sat quietly while Mrs. Diller complained. Once she threw a questioning glance at Stephanie. The child sat near the door, arms folded, both hands holding her coat lapels. Stephanie arched her eyebrows in some kind of possible secret response to her mother.

When there was a pause, Alicia moved in from where she stood just outside the cracked door. The principal looked up. Alicia said, "Mark took her coat to jump rope with."

"Is that why you did this?" the principal asked Stephanie.

"He threw it on the top of the portable," Alicia said.

"You see," Mrs. Breaks said to Mrs. Diller.

The principal cleared her throat. "I don't approve of children fighting on the playground."

As if fighting any place else would have been sanctioned.

Stephanie said, "I didn't fight."

"Was there a fight?" inquired Mrs. Breaks to the principal.

"No...er...What I meant to ask was why you, Stephanie, knocked Mark down. Was it because he took your coat?"

"I was on the slide," Stephanie said, twisting her shoe with her ankle, her head to one side, looking at no one.

"It was an accident?" the principal asked.

"How could it have been an accident?" said Mrs. Diller. "Look at Mark's face and arms. It's outrageous."

Mrs. Breaks was silent.

"I was on the slide," said Stephanie. "He was in the wrong place."

"Was it an accident?" The principal wanted that established.

"You can't stop on the slide. He didn't slide all the way. He was on the slide, and I came down. Boom!" She twisted her arm. "He fell."

That was in October.

Ruth, a little brown-haired girl who quizzed me every day, expected more to happen.

"What are they doing now?" She asked me almost daily.

I pointed to Alicia and Stephanie playing tether ball, or four square, or turning and twisting on the monkey bars. It was not until a month later that Denise Spicer's arm was broken on the monkey bars, after Denise and Cheryl Breaks had a ball fight. They were playing two square, and Denise slammed the ball, causing it to hit Cheryl in the mouth.

Denise said Cheryl was out and wouldn't switch places.

Cheryl said she was not out, because they'd agreed before the game that there'd be no slamming.

Cheryl got mad and hit the ball really hard, and it hit Denise on the chin. After that they ran around the play court, each in turn throwing the ball, hitting each other on the head, face, or anywhere the ball landed.

I arrived in time to hear Stephanie in the crowd of students who followed them. Her voice came above the shouts of others. "Denise Spicer, stop hitting my damn sister, you bitch."

"Don't call me a bitch," Denise said. "She started it!"

Bam! The ball struck Cheryl's middle.

I yelled at them to hold it, but they kept going, running and throwing the ball at each other, until soon recess was over. Cheryl was crying when she came to class.

Ruth said, "Stephanie will get you, Denise. You're in trouble!"

But Stephanie didn't pick a fight with Denise.

Instead they became friends. They played tether ball together, and the children were surprised to see how well Denise played; she won most of the games. After school, the two friends walked home together, eating ice cream cones that Stephanie bought.

But on the playground, accidents happen, even among friends. When Stephanie and Denise were playing on the monkey bars, their legs became entangled. Denise fell into the sand pit, yelling and crying. Nobody knew at first what was wrong.

"What's wrong?" I asked after clearing the children off to the side.

"My arm!" yelled Denise.

I could see the arm was bent at an unnatural angle. One of the teachers came up and said, "My God, the child's arm is broken."

Denise came back to school two days later, her arm in a cast. Before class the two girls met with their mothers in the principal's office. The door was open. Denise started to cry softly as she told it, pointing across the room with the good arm.

"She jumped on my back, and my arm twisted. And it hurts."

Denise's mother stared at Stephanie as if she expected an explanation. The principal said, "Why did you do it, Stephanie?"

Stephanie shrugged her shoulders, looked straight ahead, and said nothing.

"I heard about her," Mrs. Spicer said, pointing to Stephanie.

"Heard about who?" said Mrs. Breaks.

"That girl, there."

"'That girl there has a name." Mrs. Breaks paused. "Stephanie has had accidents like other children."

"This is no accident," said Mrs. Spicer.

"We're friends," said Stephanie. "Aren't we friends, Denise?"

Denise looked at her mother, then at her shoes. "We were friends."

"I've seen them together on the playground," the principal offered.

"Yes, I know," said Denise's mother. "She came to the house and all, but it's not real. This proves it."

"I don't understand," said Mrs. Breaks. "Cheryl told me Stephanie gave Denise ice cream cones and played tether ball with her every day."

"Can the children go out?" said Denise's mother. The principal sent them both out to wait in the secretary's office.

"Your child doesn't forgive, Mrs. Breaks," Denise's mother said. "Denise had a fight with your other daughter, Cheryl, two or three weeks ago. Stephanie is sneaky. She's hurt other children in the past. I have talked to other mothers. All that coming over to our house and buying ice cream for Denise was just some trick to catch Denise unawares."

Mrs. Breaks said, "My children are very close and protective of one another. But this looks like an accident."

"There have been far too many accidents," said the principal.

"I wish I knew her full family background," said Denise's mother.

"I see," said Mrs. Breaks, as though she was taking note of something.

When the children came back, in a stern voice Mrs. Breaks demanded, "Stephanie, did you break Denise's arm because of Cheryl?"

"Because of Cheryl what, Mom?"

"You know. Because she and Cheryl had the ball fight."

Stephanie looked straight at Denise, and a cold smile flitted across her face. She turned a harder stare on Denise's mother for just an instant. Then she looked at her own mother and in a measured, respectful voice said, "Mother, that was weeks ago. Denise and I are friends."

Mrs. Breaks looked around the room with a triumphant sweep. "You see. It was an accident. Now, tell us your side of it, dear. Go ahead, Stephanie. Tell us how it happened."

"We were playing tether ball, but I can play better than she can. She got tired and said, 'Let's go to the monkey bars. I'll show you how to skin the bear.'"

"Skin the bear?"

"You know, hang on with your arms and send your legs and the rest of your body through your arms with your head hanging down. Denise does it better than anyone. I can't do it yet. She was like this, and I was higher up. I tried it, but I didn't see her. I slipped and fell on her back, and I heard her arm go click. Like that." She turned her wrists up suddenly in a snap. Then she shrugged and looked all around.

Mrs. Breaks was satisfied, but Mrs. Spicer left the conference shaking her head.

Denise was popular. She and her friends convinced a lot of students not to play with Stephanie. Stephanie didn't seem to mind. The next few days she moved almost alone on the playground except for Alicia and Cheryl. Two things brought the children back.

Alicia was liked by almost everyone, so other children always talked to her. Since she was with Stephanie, the children gradually played with both of them. And Stephanie was the best tether ball player in the whole school. When she sent the ball whirling around the pole, her long arms followed the rope and ball almost all the way around the pole. She whisked up and down the pole so fast, and with such ease, that when the ball became tangled, it seemed she was a ballet dancer, and the ball and rope were her partners.

Children stood around frustrated at the tether ball. She frequently won games against Kathy Doyle and Jan Perkins, then Ling Sing, Noelle Kovasky, and Betty Johnson. They lost, then stood aside watching her with envy while she played Cheryl and Alicia. Alicia was sure to win if there was a girl next in line that Alicia could defeat.

"She only gives her friends chances," mumbled Betty Johnson.

That week Stephanie had two teeth out in front. Robbie Kaiser came by the tether ball game and saw it.

"Ha, ha, yo! Look at old Stephanie's teeth." And later, "Stephanie's teeth are like her grandmother's."

Stephanie liked Robbie, but she said, "Better stop it, Robbie."

"She'll get you, Robbie," Ruth warned.

But Robbie was eleven, tall, almost the largest boy in school, and nobody there fought him. He'd had a fight with a junior high school boy during baseball practice and beat him. He came by Stephanie with a football in his hand.

"Stephanie's teeth are gaped like a garage door."

She seemed glad of the attention Robbie was giving her—as long as a lot of children were not around. But then things changed. Robbie made a poem about her teeth. Children laughed with him.

"Teeth like her mother.

A face like a cow.

Teeth like a grandma.

How's that, now?"

"I told you, Robbie." Stephanie looked at him sternly. She turned red when other children ran across the playground giggling.

"She'll get you, Robbie," Ruth said, the brown-haired girl who was always looking for something to happen.

"Gap teeth, oh! Look at that doorway," yelled Robbie.

The next day at the after-lunch recess, I was standing near the portables watching some children do wind-sprint practice for field day. My glance landed on Alicia and Stephanie playing tether ball. At the same, I saw Robbie Kaiser come out of the lunchroom door and head their way. Stephanie ignored Robbie until he came near, then she gave the ball a powerful stroke that sent it whirling around the hard metal pole. She waited until it had the right speed, then she took a running start around the pole, leapt up, caught the string, and rode the ball with her legs drawn back. When she came upon Robbie passing close by the tether ball circle, one leg flew out. I heard a soft dull sound as his head flew back.

Robbie grabbed his face.

By this time I had reached him and was trying to see how badly he was hurt. He had his hand in front of his face, feeling around in his mouth as though he couldn't believe what had just happened.

Two teeth were gone, another was broken, and he had bloody gums.

Stephanie was still in the circle, whirling the tether ball. I couldn't imagine how such damage could be done to Robbie's face from one blow.

Until I looked at Stephanie's shoes: what kids called waffle stompers with hard, plastic, corrugated soles. They'd been popular some years back and were still sold at thrift stores.

I took Robbie's arm to guide him inside to the nurse.

A crowd of children milled around. One of them yelled, "Gee, Stephanie, you didn't have to kill him.

And somebody else: "I told you, Robbie. I told you."

Robbie cried. I stuffed some tissue into his hand, which he held under his dripping mouth. On the long walk across the playground to the nurse's office, children followed us. As we went through the door into the building, I looked back to see if Stephanie realized the seriousness of what had happened. She didn't look our way.

She and Alicia were whirling the tether ball.

CHERRON

PARENTS TELL KIDS TO AVOID DRUGS. How can you avoid something that's everywhere?

It was all around the campuses. The shit was everywhere and it was impossible to escape it. You hear a lot. I heard "gateway." Anything could be a gateway to using something more dangerous. If you smoked cigarettes, if you puffed a joint once, if you ate cookies laced with chronic, or sipped punch with alcohol in it.

I wanted to avoid drugs. And I tried but I couldn't live my life in fear and isolation. I had to try something sometime, and when I did, that was it. After trying it led to something else, opened a second doorway, and I just kept going, and I was lucky to be almost finishing high school with good marks. I figured I had it all mapped out. I was always a good student. I did the homework. I was interested and I didn't plan to let anybody drag me away from my goals. As for trying stuff, I didn't plan on trying. Nothing. Even in science I was never too keen on experiments unless I was sure of a safe outcome.

But you have to say hello to people, and one thing sometimes leads to another. But I thought I knew who to avoid. The biggest mistake of my life was just being civil and saying hi to Cree.

Everybody knew Cree. She hung around the high schools. At this time, I was going to Garfield. She was always in the halls or on the grounds or in the small park or parking lot. Security ran her and the guys with her off, but soon they'd all come back with some reason for being there, which was no reason at all. Cree hung out with these guys who came in from Oakland, Riverside, or Fremont or anywhere else in California. They did everything but go to class.

I went to school every day. I didn't cut class to watch soaps or smoke weed or do crack. I didn't like bad actors or people in trouble, and I sprinted away from any melee. They had these rap sessions on campus. I understood some rap, but I wasn't into it. I thought fun was in my future. I needed to get somewhere first, and that's what I was concentrating on.

But there was this wild bunch that you had to avoid, or they just kind of slipped upon you. And before you knew it, you were in their herd. I didn't know half of what I thought I knew, and before I knew it, my grades were slipping.

I didn't know how deep Cree was in this mess. I learned all this later from Denise.

"Cherron, I see you're with them now."

"With whom?" I was still high on the grade list and being myself.

"That California crowd."

"I didn't know I was with them."

"Yeah, you even eat lunch on the fringe of that group. You know Cree is their girl and procurer."

"What does that mean?"

"Don't you know all about her?"

"No, what about her?"

"She's in with all of them."

"What do you mean, in?"

"Don't you ever notice anything besides your algebra books? Don't you see what she wears?"

I had noticed these handkerchiefs. When she wore something different, she'd have this red bandana one day around her waist. The next day there would be a blue one hanging from her belt. And she was pierced everywhere. Little silver balls hung from her tongue, and she had tattoos on her behind that you could see to the side of her crack whenever she leaned over. I just thought she was flipping about as usual. Then I noticed at the barbecue that she wore the Crips headscarf. At the game between Garfield and Franklin, she wore the Bloods headscarf.

I asked Denise what that meant. How can Cree be with both groups? They are enemies and they sometimes kill each other.

"Sometimes they don't. Cree has been corded into both groups."

"Corded in?"

Denise shook her head at my ignorance. "Girl, you got to be smart but you're so dumb. 'Corded in' means she's sexing both groups. I hear they have run a train over her."

I stood there unbelieving, my mouth open in surprise.

"Girl, you'd better stop looking at your shoelaces and look up toward the sky. These people are going to take you if you aren't careful."

"Just tell me more about 'corded in'? How is that?"

"That's where the whole gang, the brothers are initiated there. You know like a fraternity. They take you to a garage or a basement, and the whole gang runs a sex train over you."

"Sex train?"

"Girl, you so dumb." Denise bent her head to the side, looking under-eyed with pity. "Everybody in the gang gets to screw you."

"What! You mean all of them? At once?"

"Yep. Melanie told me she saw Cree right after it happened." Denise giggled. "Cree's eyes were bugging out, her hair was all limp with sweat, sticking to the sides of her head. Her legs were wobbly and unsteady, her lips bruised and bleeding, and her panties were all torn, hanging off one leg. Her skirt was dirty, twisted, and ragged. All the guys were laughing how she'd sucked everybody's dicks and fucked everybody. Now they trust and love her. She's in."

I couldn't believe all this at first, but found out later it was the way it was done. "Corded in." I never was.

Cree had this beat-up old Datsun that was always full of her homies. She had a driver's license. She'd just turned sixteen, and she was all over everywhere. And Cree was in the middle of the homies. Sometimes she wore the red and white of the Bloods, and sometimes the blue and white of the Crips. She was always out in the front at barbecues or games, dealing and throwing up her hands, twisting her fingers, flashing signs. As I told you, I didn't know all this at first.

In my junior year, I had a 3.8 average and was on track to graduate until I met this guy at the Franklin/Garfield game. If you've ever been to one of those games, you know it's the biggest and craziest football mess you'd ever want to see. Brothers fight if somebody says something about a team or player, or yell when the wrong team scores. That's why Security is strict about not letting in anyone who they know causes trouble. They either can't come in, or they're thrown out at the least sign of trouble. But you can't really keep people apart who are determined to fight. Like you can't keep people apart who are meant to love each other

At the game these guys sitting behind our group of juniors kept talking about somebody being fine. I didn't really listen to them and kept watching the game, but old girl Denise who I went around with kept telling me to listen.

"They are rapping, and it sounds good." Somebody got the ball, broke into the open, and ran through tacklers, leaving them on the ground. This dude behind me was rapping about the runner, and he had this rhythm of the play. We were laughing with him. Then I heard my name in the rapping, and I thought it just sounded like my name, Cherron, but old girl Denise said, "Cherron, he's rapping about you. He knows you."

I didn't look around, but Denise acted as if she'd dropped something and bent down so she could look back at them. She straightened up, caught my arm, and acted like she was looking for someone higher up in the stands. That's when she saw him and said, "Oh, Cherron, he's fine, and he's rapping your name. You better look, girl."

I didn't look. But I kept wondering how he knew my name. I said, "Denise, you can stay here if you want to. But, girl, I'm gone." I went out and she did follow. It was the half. We went by the majorettes to the stands and got some chips. When we were coming back, I was determined to sit somewhere else, but we met Cree and some of her buddies. She just kept on talking and hugging on me and looking up in the stands and saying, "Cherron, there's someone you ought to meet. He's wild about you, girl."

"Who knows me?"

"Somebody asked me about you and begged me to tell him about you, and I did." Denise and I exchanged looks.

"Why did you do that, Elizabeth?" I called Cree by her real name so she'd know I didn't like her telling anybody about me.

"He likes you so much. He's from Compton. That's in California. He knows my family and he's cool. And he's fine like you, so the two of you need to square off and go head to head in the ring together."

"Girl, you don't know me well enough to line me up with anyone."

I was really pissed, because I knew that's the way things started. You didn't know some fool from Adam and then suddenly you were tangled with them.

Denise and I sat somewhere else in the stands. That game was exciting, and they always have a band after the big game, so we wanted to go to the dance. This boy I knew was talking to me. When we passed through the door, he was high-fived by a couple of his friends. He said, "Wait a minute, Cherron," and I stood there near him.

When Cree came up with these guys, Denise nearly broke my ribs with her elbow in my side and whispering, "That's him. The one on the left. His name is Drake."

He was dressed pretty sharp, with these pointed-toe shoes all shined, and a cool shirt with no collar that hung around him nicely. His hair was combed back. He was different and didn't talk a lot. He just listened; just watched me and let his buddies talk. Cree was going on a mile a minute. His buddies rushed me for dances, but he didn't. I was curious why he didn't ask me to dance. I wasn't spectacular, but I could zip in and out and do what was popular, because Denise and I and some other girls used to dance at Denise's house. I did find it kind of comforting looking at Drake who was not hyper.

After the dance he came with Cree over to Denise's, where we hung out. I didn't like any of the guys there; they were Cro-Magnons who only wanted to show their popularity at somebody else's expense, and call people bitches and whores, and yell obscenities at each other. They were so in love with themselves, and they rushed you with their hands all over you, disrespecting you as a woman. Nobody invited them. They just came. Denise had her eye on one of them, and she invited them in.

I said right there in her ear, "Denise, you don't know these guys. You're always telling me to be careful, and look at you! That's how things start. Because my mother worked for the YWCA and she schooled me about guys and their behaviors. I am going home, girl."

But she said, "Come on, Cherron. Don't leave me alone. Please stay and let's have fun."

Soon after that, I was serving punch when Drake took a glass. He said to his friend nearby, "You tell her to pardon me. I don't know how to talk to her, but I sure would like a minute of her time."

I didn't say anything, but later we did dance. He wanted to tell me about his sister and his life in Compton. He played basketball. He was a senior in high school. He flew up with some cousins, and he liked it, so he might stay. I asked him why he might stay. He looked at me and smiled.

And that was it. He had a nice outward smile.

"I'm beginning to like Seattle." He said it like that, smiling down at me. He was tall, with these beautiful white teeth and a genuine smile. After we danced a second time, Cree called me in the back and got very familiar. She said, "He likes you, Cherron."

After that night I did see him at school in the hallway. He didn't go back to Compton. We started talking and being around each other. I still didn't know anything about Cree. All the stuff I'd heard about her didn't seem to match with her as a person. I did not realize it then, but something stopped my mind from engaging, kept me from thinking right.

Drake was heavily into music and had a lot of friends. Cree was the girlfriend of one of them, so she and I went around together. I broke my rules and went to a number of parties, and began kissing with Drake. Then he asked me to go down to Compton, where I could stay in my own hotel and meet his folks and his friends. I had never been anywhere.

Yes, I blanked out all the signals that tried to tell me something was wrong. I told myself I wanted to do something for myself. I thought about it in the library one day when I was working an algebra problem. I just flapped the book shut, got out of there, and went to the bank.

I had my own money in the bank, which I'd earned from my own job. I bought my own plane ticket. The band had a trip planned, and I told my mother I was going with the band. She said that would look good as an extra class activity on my application for college. She didn't even check up on me. Cree went with her guy, and we just kicked it together. I met a select few of his friends.

When we were back in Seattle, Drake and I were very tight, and that was the beginning of my problems. I suppose he shielded me from what he was really like.

Cree lived with her Aunt Tea. I skipped school one day and went over to Cree's and met Drake there. After that I'd do it twice a week, and then for more days. I am not proud to say he was more interested in me than he was in school. I learned more about him as he began to commute every week to Compton. He was a big important Crip who made trips to Mexico. By the time I learned this, I was in love too deep with him and didn't know how to stop myself.

When we went to Aunt Tea's house, she didn't care. She never asked us about school. She was into photography and spent all her time at the house developing something in her darkroom. She'd let us into the house and then disappear. If she had to run out to deliver pictures or something, she hurried out with the admonition: "Don't go near my darkroom." Cree would not let anybody in there, saying, "My aunt will kill me if I ever let anybody in her darkroom. A friend went in there by mistake. He didn't stay but a minute, but my aunt put me out of her house. I had to crash wherever I could for more than a month and beg her to let me in here again. I don't ever want to do that again."

Anyway I had fun with Cree and saw what life was like, but I failed two classes. Then Drake went down to Compton one week and didn't come back on Sunday evening. We waited and waited until we found he got himself killed in Mexico. I was in shock and didn't talk to anyone for weeks.

For the first time in my life, I spoke meanly to my mother, and she couldn't tell me anything that I wanted to hear. She said, "Girl, you're crazy. You think you the first woman in the world ever went crazy over a man?" I told her she never had a special man. We fought day and night.

By the time the year was over, I didn't graduate, and I came to this alternative school to take makeup classes after one term. When I graduate, I can transfer to any school.

But then I had other problems. Cree wanted to follow me into the alternative school. After what happened, I figured I owed her. You know the policy: If you are a student, you can recommend other students. She wanted me to recommend her to come in, which I did.

When the counselor gave Cree the slip showing how many credits she had, I was flabbergasted. I'd never seen her go to classes at Garfield, and I didn't know what middle school she came from, but she had ten credits, which meant she was a junior. That put her on track to graduate a year after me. I didn't see her much at school, because I had this job with the bank, and if I kept up my grades, they were going to give me a scholarship to college. I went to class every day and to work every evening.

I did not know what was coming down. But then Denise told me some more news.

"Girl, did you hear about Cree?" Denise had graduated on time, and she was in the community college.

"No. What's that?"

"She can't do the work. She's getting bad grades."

"Maybe she's running around with the gangs."

"You know most of those guys are in jail."

"What's the matter?"

"They're investigating her school records. They say she came from Mercer."

I saw Cree on weekends. She came by the job and waited in the bank lobby, because we close early on Saturday.

She wanted to hang out, but I wasn't interested. We went to the Galleria near Westlake Mall, where everybody hangs out. We talked several times in the food circus, high up there. I said, "What's this about you not cutting it at the alternative school? And they are searching through your records at Mercer."

She blurted out, "Aunt Tea is tight with the custodian at Mercer. He shifts around at schools and he owes Aunt Tea a favor."

If she'd told me Aunt Tea was tight with a counselor or the superintendent, I'd have been impressed. But tight with a custodian? I didn't see the importance, and she dismissed everything with the phrase, "I got all that shit covered." Then she shook her leg up and down the way she did when she was agitated. "They can't do a fucking thing."

When she talked like that and moved the tray about on the table, it meant something was bugging her. So I pressed on.

"Are they looking at other schools you went to? What's up with that?"

"They looked up my records at Arbor Heights, but that's cool. Aunt Tea is on it, see? And she'll look after me as long as I help her. Are you getting over Drake? I know that was hard, but I know another guy who could help you forget."

"I don't need anybody to help me forget him. I'm back doing my own thing. But about you and your records. I don't get it. What is—"

She cut me off. "Let's just say Aunt Tea can fix anything. Ever have any trouble, just let me know."

"But if you can't do the work, how is Aunt Tea going to cover for you at school?"

"Look, I am doing the work. What is important is for me to be in school, and I am there, okay?"

I couldn't get any more out of her, so we dropped it.

Two weeks later we had a holiday. Kids were out of school, and we ended up at her house, sitting around watching soaps. I smoked a joint with her, something I'd never done and had promised myself I'd never do. She was doing 'shrooms, got spaced out, talking all funky. Then she conked out on the sofa. I got up from the couch to go pee. The house was almost dark, with no lights on.

And I stumbled into the wrong room. I turned on the light, searching for the mirror and commode. My head was woozy. I wanted to laugh, but then damn! I was in Aunt Tea's darkroom. Oh shit, I looked around for Cree. I had forgotten she was conked out on the couch, and I thought she'd know I was here in Aunt Tea's darkroom. Then I got to looking at the walls. A wire stretched against one wall over some double sinks, with clothes pins holding pictures on it. An infrared light burned in a corner over a long table that held trays and printing fluid in plastic cans. Down the table, past the printing trays, pictures lay in piles. Next to them were credit cards, all filled out but blank where the names should be. And ID badges waiting for names and passport-sized pictures.

My first thought was to get the hell out as quickly as possible, but there was something familiar about some of the pictures. I flipped through a few, and yes there were shots of kids I knew from Garfield.

Then there was me with Drake. We were making out in Cree's room. Then—whoa! One with Drake's head—Dead Drake—with his head down between my legs and me with this funny look on my face. I was totally naked with my head thrown back to the side.

I was so shocked, like I'd been hit hard in the face. I grabbed at that picture and almost crumpled it up. There was another of Denise, and what was it in her mouth but her boyfriend's thing. I rubbed over it trying to brush it off. There were many pictures of me, which I took and pushed it up my blouse. On the floor there were magazines I'd never seen on the newsstands. *Hustler*, yes, but there were others. The women were all show-ing their stuff and in different poses.

I thought I heard Cree. I stopped short and listened, but it was a car passing outside.

I wanted to destroy all of the pictures, but right then, I had to get out of there. I turned off the light and tiptoed out quietly, thinking Cree could wake up and see me there. In the bathroom next door, I breathed deeply, holding the sides of the face bowl. I squatted and while peeing, suddenly I needed to do number two and it seemed my whole insides came out, just runny and lots of gas. I vomited in the toilet, then I ran cold water in my cupped hands and dunked my whole face in it. That was like getting a fresh life. And then I flushed the toilet.

Cree woke up and rushed in. She looked at me funny-like and said, "Oh, how long was I out?"

I tried to be calm, feeling the print of the pictures under my blouse as I washed and dried my hands. My heart was beating so loud and fast, it seemed anyone could hear it.

"Oh, just a minute or two before I came in here."

She looked all around, satisfied. I soon made an excuse and left.

What was Aunt Tea but a fucking criminal and a pornographer getting rich off kids, selling their pictures to smut magazines, and selling fake IDs, passports, and credit cards? She and Cree were criminals, and I was from time to time living in their house, recommending Cree to my school. She was having sex with Crips and Bloods, and a boy was killed. I was lucky to be alive, so I told Cree I had to go home and clean the house on the weekend.

She said, "You can't just go. I have some more bud, and we can hang. Just stay here for the rest of the day. Aunt Tea won't be back until tomorrow. She went to Redding to deliver something. She left in a hurry and told me the usual. 'Don't go in my darkroom.'"

"We won't," I said, and I got out of there.

That was the best I could do. I tried to get all the pictures, but I thought Aunt Tea would have the negatives somewhere. And if I took them, she'd know I'd seen everything. I knew then Aunt Tea was dangerous. As it was, I didn't think she'd be so quick to sell my pictures, since Cree and I went around together. But whenever I think of all the things Drake and I did in that room, the drugs and all, she would not be afraid to sell pictures, because she could stop us from talking by showing us a few photographs of what we did.

Anyway I never went back, and I avoided Cree after that, but I told old girl Denise about it, and she said I shouldn't worry, because she had friends who'd take care of it.

I said, "Denise, don't be stupid."

She said, "What? I am not going near there, but I can guarantee something will happen."

Anyway, they found out Cree had good grades everywhere, but she couldn't do the high school work. After one term they kicked her out.

Just before I graduated, a fire broke out in Aunt Tea's. She was out of town, and Cree was not there either. A water main broke behind Aunt Tea's house while the firemen were using their fire axes on the darkroom windows, and all of Aunt Tea's pictures and darkroom stuff were destroyed by the firemen who broke windows and trampled on everything

When I heard that, I laughed. I rang up Denise on the phone and said, "Thank you, girl."

She laughed and said, "I have no idea what you're talking about."

Somehow she'd made it happen, but knowing Denise, she's never going to own it. I graduated, and I'm getting that scholarship from the bank. I hope all of that is behind me.

From time to time I go in stores and look at those sex magazines, looking to see if I am in one of them. Sometimes in the stores when I am turning the pages on the rack, I look around to see who is watching me. I look at the centerfold, wondering if some time I'll see my open self there on a page with that dead boy's head down there between my legs. If anybody chances to see me then, with these magazines spread out on the racks in Borders or in Barnes and Nobles, they'd think I was a sex maniac.

ELEVATED

KATIE MADISON GOT IN THE elevator on the seventh floor of The Elton Electronics Building, headed for a snack. She was working late tonight and she was hungry. It was 4:15. She had to be back before the building closed at 5:00 p.m. Just as the elevator door closed, Steve Curtin's well-groomed head and his smiling white teeth flashed in the doorway.

Of the several others in the elevator, Katie was closest to the control panel and could have touched the button to have the door open to let him in, but she didn't move. When the elevator swiftly descended, she felt elated that he had not got the chance to ride down. Several girls from her office liked him, fawned over him. Katie couldn't see why. It was plain to her that he was a jerk, stuck on himself. He brushed by her one morning when she was late, jumping in front of her and not holding the door.

Then at the office workshop, during the working luncheon, he'd refused to work with her group. Besides, he had kicked her handcrafted leather purse under the eraser board and said aloud, "Oops, somebody left their old leather trunk out of place."

Katie thought that was rude and swore to herself that she'd never speak to him again.

She grabbed a Reuben sandwich and several chocolates at Starbucks. She thought of getting a latté, but there was coffee in the office. She hurried out with her purchases. Just as she approached her building, wouldn't you know, she saw Steve Curtin coming out of the bar next door, heading toward the building again.

"Behind in your work, Mr. Curtin," she thought. "Katie Madison is never late in her work, thank you." She congratulated herself. "Tomorrow, I'll be in New Jersey, attending my best friend's wedding."

The last people were just leaving the building when she got to the door ahead of Steve Curtin. The guard standing there with the key. "You'll be the only two in the building."

They both entered the elevator, and she immediately pushed number seven. Steve went to a neutral corner. The elevator did not start at once, it paused with the door open. Katie looked all around, then stuck her head a little way out to see if anyone had come up and was controlling the panels from outside. Then there was a whir, and the door quickly closed. The elevator moved up, running slowly as if it was tired, not the zip as it usually did. Katie glanced around at Steve. She noticed he was in pants, shirt, no coat, and his tie was still tight around his neck.

The number display read 5. The elevator stopped, but the door did not open. Steve was looking at her this time. "Something is wrong with it," he said. He moved as if he was going to try to open the control panel. There was no phone in it.

"Don't you dare bother that," she said.

He hit his pocket and got a solid flap sound.

"I could call them before they leave the building if I had my cell phone. It's being charged in the office."

She held her right hand with her leather purse away from him, and in her left hand was the bag holding the sandwich and chocolates. "Mine is on my desk upstairs."

They stood in the elevator, looking up and all around, and listening.

Steve went to the door and tried his hand on the little vertical slit where the door usually parted to open.

Then he surveyed the panel. "Sometimes there is a phone right about here in elevators." There was a switch near the panel. He looked at her. "I just want to turn this off and on to see if it will attract attention or if it will affect the elevator."

"Go ahead," she said, watching his every move.

He flipped the switch off and on a couple of times. The lights in the elevator went off and on. The switch controlled the light in the ceiling of the elevator.

He left it alone then and yelled up at the ceiling. "The elevator is stuck. We are trapped in the elevator." He heard his echo and said, "Trapped," several times. "Trapped in the elevator."

She smiled, looked down and said, "Good results." The whole build-ing was silent, except for the whir and distant roar of an engine somewhere below them.

"Maybe we had better get our territorial boundaries." she said. "Mr. Curtin, I am going to remain near the control panel. I suggest you pick another corner."

"What? Er...Yes. All right. I understand."

She could hear him mumbling something to himself. And he said it several times.

"Did you intend me to hear that, or is it another insult?"

"Insult? Oh, I don't know what you mean. I said I wish I hadn't had those two beers."

Katie hadn't followed his thoughts, "Oh, you drank beers in that bar outside? "

"Yes, I did."

He went to a corner at the back of the elevator, diagonally across from Katie. Near the control panel, a little metal box held printed brochures and had a sign: "Take one." Steve walked up. Katie turned quickly, not know-ing the meaning of his movements.

"I just wanted to read one of these." He pulled down one of the bro-chures and went back to his corner. Then putting his back against the wall, moving his feet slowly out, he slid down to a sitting position in the corner.

She watched him over her shoulder. She hit on the door several times with the flat of her hand. "Do you think the guards and everyone have left the building?" she said.

"It appears so. I worked here once before, and there was a note that said, 'Don't put anything in front of the door. It locks automatically.'"

He paused awhile, then said, "When you leave after working late, you can't get back in even if you forgot something."

"I can't stay here all night. I have to be in New Jersey tomorrow."

"Maybe you're going to fly out of here in that magic handmade leather trunk."

"It's just my luck to be trapped in an elevator with the office jerk." She glared at him.

It got quiet after that. Katie resigned herself to spending a night there for there was little chance that anyone would come. Of course there was the possibility that the elevator itself would just start working again, on its own. She stood up and punched seven and then one. No response; just a click, a hum, then silence. She slid down and sat with her head on her purse. She thought she might eat her sandwich, but she began suddenly to think of their position and how practical it was to eat for it might cause a reaction in her stomach, and for the first time she was alarmed. What if she needed to go to the bathroom, badly? Thinking of this and going over how she could still make it to New Jersey if someone let them out of the elevator by eight o'clock tomorrow morning, she must have dozed off. She awoke with a jerk. It was colder in the elevator. And she heard Steve calling to her from his corner.

"Katie, I…I have a serious problem. I have been sitting here thinking. I got up and walked around and now… I'm standing one foot on the other. And…I…oh, no. I'll just wait to tell you…"

"What in the world are you talking about?"

"It's embarrassing, and I don't want to disrespect you. But it's serious, and we don't know how long we will be in here."

"Until morning at the latest. What's wrong with you? Is Mr. Know-it-all going to cry? Don't worry, your reputation is safe."

"It's both of our reputations and health that I'm thinking of."

She looked at him. He was sweating and moving about as if he was anxious and in pain. "Why, Steve what in the world is wrong with you? I hope you are not sick, because I am no good as a nurse."

"I don't need a nurse, but I do need compassion."

"You need something that you yourself cannot give?" She almost laughed out loud.

He caught at his pants between his legs and leaned forward. "I have been trying to tell you that I…I, well, I have to make water. I've got to pee."

She almost laughed, but then it struck her how awkward. They were in an elevator. How was that to be accomplished?

She turned her back on him then. "Er…Just go ahead."

"Go ahead? You know I can't."

"If you've got to, you got to. You can't hold it?"

"No. I drank two beers, and I am bursting. I've got to go."

"But go where? All you have is your corner."

"I… can't do that. It will smell. It may run out to other floors. And when they open the door…"

"But you can't help it. Better go ahead."

"Katie, it may leak and run out in the building somewhere."

"What else can you do? You've got to," Katie said.

"I can't hold it much longer. I want to negotiate something with you," Steve said.

"With me? You aren't serious. What?"

"Think about this, quickly. Your purse is made of leather."

"My purse! Hell no! What are you suggesting?" It dawned on Katie that it was probably the only sensible solution. "I had this purse made. And after what you said, the insult."

He came wobbly over toward her. She retreated, the purse held firmly against her body, away from him.

"I can get you another one when we get out," he pleaded.

She saw his face then, kind of grey, and he was sweating profusely. He kept on talking. "It is probably waterproof and will not let it leak out. Please let me use it, and we won't have this car all smelly and disgraceful when they open it to let us out."

In that instant Katie knew it was the only logical thing to do. She opened her purse and took her personal things out, placing them in the bag with the sandwich and the chocolates. She removed her makeup kit, her wallet and phone book, a notepad, and some receipts. She usually cleaned out her purse and did not have much in it. She noted that the purse had a double lining and she had some Kleenex in it. She handed it over to Steve with her back to him.

He went back to his neutral corner and she tried not to listen, but she heard anyway the "Is…Is…Is.…See" stream as he peed into her purse.

She kept her eyes diverted. She heard him zip up the purse and snap the two handles together. When she finally looked, he held the purse in his hands as though he was about to return it to her. She quickly turned away. He seemed relaxed. He put the purse aside and did not say anything, but a muffled, "Thanks."

His voice sounded relieved. A few minutes later she heard his even breathing. In a few minutes, she caught herself nodding off. She changed her position so that she leaned her head against the wall. She got up then and tried the switches again. She clicked the light off and on and hit the buttons alternately for each floor. All her efforts were followed by silence. She sat down, leaning her head against the wall where she could see Steve in his corner, sleeping. She tried to stay awake, but nodded off anyway.

She woke up feeling pressure in her loins. She felt chilled. At home she was not used to waking up to go to the bathroom at night, but now she needed to go. It was not urgent. She looked at her watch. It was 2:24 a.m.

She tried to go back to sleep and she did succeed in drifting off to sleep, but each time the coldness in the elevator brought her back to an abrupt consciousness. She needed to go now, and it was more urgent than before. She decided not to give in, and it'd probably go away. But in the next hour she awoke dreaming she was in her own bathroom sitting on the commode. She had almost believed it and almost let go. She was ashamed. It would've been all over her under things. She had to be careful. She was awakened twice more with the pressure in her bladder more urgent than before. She knew now it was best to do it, while he was asleep. She thought about the physical position she had to assume. She also remembered she had to retrieve the purse and use the same purse he'd used — real intimacy. She shuddered and withdrew in distaste. But her body demanded she do it! So, she stole quietly over to him, only to find the purse's handles were entangled with his fingers. She'd wanted to take it and use it while he slept and put it back, and he wouldn't know. Now, she had to awaken him and ask for it back, so she could do what he'd done.

But then he moved, turned toward her, then turned again. She'd quickly reclaimed her place in the corner and now pretended to be asleep. He changed his position, turned his back to her and brought the purse back to use again. She heard again the squirting sound. Louder now. He closed the purse and pushed it a little distance away. He looked around him. Looked over in her direction. Then curled up in a corner of the elevator and not long. Afterwards she heard his rhythmic sleep.

Her watch said 4:50 a.m. She had to pee now. She went toward him, lifted the bag, and scuttled back to her corner. She was surprised at its heaviness. She got her panties off and over one leg. Then she opened the bag and kneeled over it, making sure the hem of her dress flared out around her legs and body. What a relief to finally let go. And to feel it flow away from her. Hearing it sing into the purse was pleasant. The odor she smelled could have been the newness of the bag or the sourness of urine. She applauded the feeling of relief in her entire body. She finished and searched in the sandwich bag beside her for a dry Kleenex or napkin when Steve moved around in the opposite corner. She had the napkin and quickly wiped before he glanced her way.

Steve looked all around, as if he was disoriented. She waved his head away, and he turned. She then brought out the purse from beneath her dress, fastened its zipper and pushed it away from her. She put her leg back in her panties, pulled her dress down, then turning away, looking away from him she curled in her corner and tried to sleep. In an hour, she thought, someone would come to open the building and then they'd open the elevator. The two of them would finally be free.

"Here," she said. "You must be hungry." She kept the chocolates and began munching on one and pushed the sandwich toward him. It slid across the elevator floor.

Steve picked it up, "Yes, I'm hungry." He unwrapped the sandwich and said, "But you should have a piece." He offered it back to her.

She shook her head. "No! I have these," and held up the chocolates and kept on eating them.

She heard him chewing. She turned her back to him and started to use her makeup kit on her face. She used Kleenex on her eyes and mouth, and put on lipstick. She stood up, her back to him, and smoothed out her wrinkled dress. Soon he moved also.

His tie had become awry during the night, and his pants had slid and twisted while he slept. She saw him brushing his shirt front, patting his pants, and rubbing his face. She handed him a Kleenex.

"I am sorry about last night," he said.

"What do you mean?"

He stammered. "About your new leather purse. I will really repay… I mean, get you another one." Both of their eyes shifted to the purse where it rested engorged on the elevator floor.

"That wasn't your fault. It was nature speaking."

"But I was too brash. Asking to relieve myself in a lady's handbag," he shook his head. "I was and I am terribly embarrassed."

"I'd never have thought it," Katie said.

"What? Why not?"

"The way you refuse to bond with others or care about what is said. Oh, and you called my purse a huge trunk at the office workshop." She looked directly at him as she spoke.

"That was silliness," he admitted. "Nobody thought I was being mean."

"I did," Katie said.

"Then I must show I am sorry. Will you let me do that if we are ever let out of this…er…prison?"

Soon after that, the elevator switched on automatically and began whirring. It ran down to the basement without stopping. The custodian stood with a surprised look when the elevator door opened, disclosing two tired people in it.

"Sorry, folks, the night custodian cut off the wrong switches. I hope you were not too inconvenienced."

Katie and Steve chose to walk up the stairs to the seventh floor.

"Are you going to work?" Steve asked.

"No, no one's in the office yet. I just have to get my cell phone and a few things, and I am going straight home. I hope I haven't missed my flight to New Jersey. How about you?"

"I'll get my cell phone. Then I am going shopping."

He carried the leather purse as if it were heavy.

SANDI

I THINK I LAUGH TOO MUCH. Sometimes I think I am in this school because I laugh so much. Nothing is really funny to me, but I laugh about
almost anything. I think that is why the counselor asked me to join Group.

I caught her watching me once in a room full of kids. I did not join in
with what they were saying, but I laughed all the while they were talking.
Then I looked up and saw her watching me. The next day she said, "Sandi,
if you need an extra elective class, I'd like it if you joined Group."

I thought maybe if I joined, I'd find out things I didn't know about
myself and stuff. Don't ask me what, but I thought maybe I'd understand
some things better. So, I registered for Group. It was not like any class I'd
been in before. Everybody just talked—about themselves. The counselor
just listened and nodded her head most of the time.

Somebody said it was a safety valve. I didn't understand that exactly,
but it was about letting off pressure or steam. I didn't have either. But I
mean, as a class with credit, Group was different. Anybody could raise a
topic and anybody could make a comment. Nobody was to criticize, just
to make observations. Sometimes some of us forgot that and criticized
what was said. But then the counselor would say, "Is that what we said we
would do, criticize each other?" And then it would stop.

My friends think I am fun to be with, but I am not fun to be by myself.
I have to brush my teeth and gargle with antiseptic or I don't feel good in
my mouth. I like my tongue to be pink. I don't want anything white on it.

Today we took our pictures for the annual. I don't like those pictures at
all. Everyone tells me that I am very beautiful—and I am a naturally
photogenic type because my eyes are blue, my face is oval, and I still

have long blonde hair that reaches down my back. But often I comb it so that much of my face is not seen. I like it better that way.

In Family Life Class, we had this assignment about pictures, writing and comparing then and now—you know pictures from your early childhood and now. I think that teacher can read me, look right through me, look at me and know all about me. He reminds me of somebody.

One day he asked me, "Were you happier in middle school?"

I almost fell off my chair. I blurted out, "Why did you ask that?"

He said, "Oh, nothing," but I thought he knew all about me. Was it because when we were comparing the pictures, I kept saying I didn't like my pictures now and did not want to look at them? We have to bring those pictures to class, those then-and-now photographs. And students have to match them and guess about each other's pictures and tell how they differ and what tipped you off to who was who. I guessed a lot of them.

But I couldn't have guessed mine. I am nothing like I was when I was twelve. I can match the one-year-old and the twelve okay, but I can't match the twelve-year-old with me now at seventeen. I have changed a lot. I don't like to look at any of my pictures now.

When kids from the office bring around a notice, they often ask me if I want to do a retake of my picture. I say, "You must be crazy, because I'd just tear them all up."

Mother complains and says they are cute.

Mother doesn't know a lot of things. I take drugs—most everything I'm offered. I don't need them or want them, but everybody includes me in everything. Even when I'd rather be left out, they call and say, "C'mon, Sandi. We're going to smoke some chronic in the yard of that apartment next to the school." I do it, because what else is there?

Everybody in our neighborhood where I live is mostly well off, rich. I guess my parents are. There are big expensive houses. I mean huge with lots of empty rooms in them. With nothing to do, my mother does a lot of charity work. "Giving back," she calls it. Some kid said, "Giving back what they stole from the poor." But mummy...Mom is a giver, and she does charity work with the Catholic sisters of the big Convent. And she encourages me to help out by running errands and mowing lawns and all.

I keep thinking of what happened in the attic of the house two doors over from ours. The grandson of the old people who lived there only came up every summer. I used to visit the old people, do chores for them, go to the store, pick up parcels for them at the post office, and cut their grass when I was eleven, twelve, and thirteen. They were mostly deaf, especially the husband. The wife wore these thick lenses. She couldn't see much, and I used to read to her, and I'd play and read in their attic.

They had a lot of interesting stuff there that as a kid I had not seen or experienced. When the grandson came up in the summer, I went up there with him, and he'd show me things, adult stuff, and tell me not to tell my parents that he'd come. He visited them for a couple of years and I was over there learning stuff from him—California stuff. He said, "I'll show you some Hollywood stuff." And he did.

But he didn't come after his grandparents died, both within days of each other. The old people had fixed it so the Catholic charity could sell anything in the house. The Mother Superior and Mom went up to the attic, and there on a sleeping bag they found panties and blouses. My mother told the Mother Superior that who ever lived there had bought blouses just like the ones I had when I was in the seventh grade.

When I heard her say that, I had to go and gargle. I needed my mouth to feel fresh.

Anyway I brought my pictures to this teacher's class for the assignment. He said I was beautiful, looking at pictures from when I was in kindergarten and fourth grade. I agreed with him. I liked the pictures from then. And I don't know when I started laughing at everything and hating the pictures of myself now. I even hate to look in the mirror. I haven't liked my pictures since the eighth grade and I don't ever want to see a picture of me in the school's annual again. I wish I could stop laughing at everything. Because nothing is really funny.

I'm not buying a copy of the annual this year.

LAMONT AND KENYATTA

LAMONT AND I JUST GOT TOGETHER right away. He didn't know anything about me, and I didn't know anything about him. We were in this class. Our chairs were in a wide circle, and he was across the room opposite to my seat.

This teacher had a way of challenging you. Not calling on you but looking at you in an accusing manner, like he was saying, "If you'd read the assignment, you could answer this question.' I didn't want him to believe I hadn't read it. We were in social studies class, and I thought I could hang with any teacher. See I was a reader and thinker, but this teacher, Mark Collins, was a friend of Hayden, the science teacher. They liked to link lessons. Collins must have discussed assignments with Hayden, so he knew we were studying Darwin's *Origin of The Species.*

He said, "Now, what did Darwin mean by survival of the fittest?"

One student said, "It's where animals or plants inherit from parents the right things that fit them into the surrounding, so they can easily get whatever they want and need to be comfortable and exist."

Collins nodded encouragement. "Did he really say that?"

Ben Anderson, that big tackle on the football team said, "It's like what Joe Kelly and Garth have when they run the football. They dominate other players and their teams. They are fit and they survive."

The teacher said, "Yes, yes, I hope you are thinking what that means individually."

This person sitting directly across from me in the circle kind of waited and raised his hand and said, "To me it means I have to think about what I need to do to make it out there. I take stock of what I've got and then try to get more. Like from my surroundings. Like get better and that way, I take it to the max, and that's how I become fit for it and survive everything. But it starts with my parents."

This girl Shelly (I didn't know anyone in the class then) didn't mind letting it all hang out, whether she was smoking a joint or what I think of her. She said, "If you know you've got your shit together, and if you... uh...mate, you pass that trait to your children, and they survive because they are fit."

Somebody else said, "No, you're not having all of it when you're born and everything. I mean it's like Lamont said, not born with it all, and that's it. You can get more, maybe of what you need."

But when we were in biology class, I had read some of *Origin of Species* by Darwin, and he didn't say anything about survival of the fittest. I looked it up on the net with that kid in my biology section, Aaron, who's a whiz on the internet, and we read all about it. It wasn't Darwin who first said that. It was an old dude who was in economics. That's my field and that's where I think it's at.

I told the class, "I read about this guy, Herbert Spencer, who thought economics was something like biology. He studied social statistics. He said free market economics was like biology where the fittest survive." Then I told them, "It's not all biology. It is about power and money, and Herbert Spencer coined the phrase Survival of the Fittest. Darwin called it natural selection."

When I finished, my hand was still up. The teacher said, "Yes, Kenyatta, you may go on."

I said, "That's what it boils down to now, and you asked how it will fit into our lives. Well, I want to go into real estate and buy property and increase my economic power. Then I can survive." I was out of breath and I just stopped. My face was glowing.

The teacher was laughing and made some remark about sharing the results of the discussion with Mr. Hayden, the biology teacher. He called for a break, and we left the classroom.

The others walked out to smoke, but I stood outside under this cherry tree with pink blossom strewn over the ground, talking to this old girl, a friend of mine, and looking at everybody. Sure enough, this boy who had exchanged looks with me in class kept on looking. He had his backpack slung over one shoulder, but he didn't smoke like the others. I kept glancing at him and talking to my old girl as if I hadn't noticed him. When he walked, he had this kind of beautiful, smooth, determined glide. I thought

I'd seen him somewhere before. There are lots of students in school, and if you go from kindergarten to first year college, you meet a great many of them. But he kept looking, and I kept glancing at him. Old girl noticed me looking and said, "Ken, I saw that."

I acted surprised. "What you talking about, girl?"

He kind of glided over and said, "I like what you said in there. And you're pretty, too."

I was looking at his mouth, because his eyes said more. I found myself wanting to go near him. I just said it was a good discussion, and he walked away with Joe and Garth and Joe. Garth looked back at me and old girl, and they laughed and hit each other's hands in joy. And old girl jabbed me with an elbow. "Somebody likes Kenyatta. Girl, who was that?"

I said, "Just someone from class."

"Un huh. Your socks are in the toes of your shoes right now?"

"Girl, what do you mean?"

"You know he zapped you. Anybody could see that."

I never knew other people could detect somebody falling in love, but old girl had done just that. He'd looked at me and said, "You're pretty, too." He hadn't hit on me or anything, just admired the scenery and stated actual facts. Other boys had said that and it didn't mean much, but this time I listened.

I had to know the dude's name after the way he looked at me, so I looked at the sign-in sheet, saw where he was sitting, and matched it with the name. Lamont. I said it softly to myself so I'd remember it. Lamont.

Then I found out who he was. What Joe Kelly and Garth were to football, he was to basketball. That's where I had seen that glide motion, for he was six feet four and slim. He hit baskets from everywhere on the court, and had hit thirty-five points in several games. His name was Lamont Darnkins. After that, we sat near each other at lunch in the atrium, and one day our lunch trays touched. Our eyes met up close, and he repeated what he'd said after that class. "Smart and pretty, too."

When I smiled, he said, "Do you know your eyes dance beautifully?"

I kept looking and laughing at him. I liked his mouth. He didn't stare, but he gave me solid looks every now and then. And we came around to discussing life. I was going into real estate when I got my degree, and he hoped to get his degrees and play pro basketball. That's what we're doing. And in just a year or two, you'll see our names out there with pro teams if you watch. Mine will be in real estate, and his will be in basketball.

LELIANA

I ACTUALLY KNEW THE COP WHO arrested me: RC Colman. We kids called him RC Cola. He was one of those who set up to trace us kids back to our suppliers of alcohol and drugs. They used us as bait to catch the meth makers and the pushers. They didn't have to worry about me there. I don't do meth. I'm no tweaker. Tweakers will do anything. I have done alcohol and marijuana. That's what RC pegged me for.

The way they did it was to put us on diversion and watch us. Diversion is when you get caught once but have no record. Instead of sending you to juvie or worse, they put you on soft probation, watch you, and have you report once a week. When we were arrested a second or third time, they threatened us with timed lockups, trying to get us to inform on our sources and our friends.

Today RC Cola arrested me for shoplifting a bag of potato chips.

"Where do you get the stuff, Leliana?"

"You can buy anything in the Red Apple Grocery Store. It's a one-stop shop," I tell him.

"You can get drugs here in the grocery?"

"If not in the store, then in the parking lot." Kids joked that meth and marijuana would soon be stacked on grocery shelves. I laughed to myself.

"But why steal just a bag of chips? I can't believe that."

"You know, you're right. No way would I get busted for a bag of chips. Look!" I pulled out cigarettes, a whole bag of M&Ms, some beef jerky, and a forty-liter bottle of beer from my big old jacket pockets. I pulled it all out. I didn't care. If you're busted, you're busted.

"Hey, hey! Whoa, what's going on? Are you really that hungry?"

"You bet your brass ass badge, I am."

He asked me a lot of questions about where I got alcohol and drugs. I told him again, "The Red Apple."

Zilch. I didn't know anything.

He said, "This is nothing. Are you taking chips and getting in deeper to spite your parents?"

Even after I showed him all the stuff I'd jacked, he was hung up on the chips! I wanted to spit in his face.

"To spite my parents. What?" I laughed at him. "Shit, I was hungry and had spent all the goddamn fucking mullah my mom gave me. I am fifteen years old and I am in charge of every fucking thing at home except the money. I rule that house." If you go vulgar on them, sometimes they are disgusted enough to leave you alone.

He said, "I know you, Leliana. You're smarter than this. You did it to spite your parents." He knew both my parents drank heavily. Oh, all right. They're alcoholics.

"Whatever!" I said.

"I know all about it. They'll be sorry to see you in juvie where I'm just locking you up. There will be a fine, and they have to come and get you. That's what you want?"

"Okay. If that's what you think."

He took me to the station. On the way I sat in his car, using the cell phone.

Dad came to get me. I don't see how they couldn't tell he was drunker than a raccoon in a garbage dump. Mother used to say that about him. He was braver than hell to drive in his condition. He'd have made a breathalyzer giddy. But he stood up straight, and he'd sprayed his mouth with something. He hardly smelled of alcohol at all.

As soon as he saw me, out of the corner of his mouth, Dad said, "What in hell did you do now? "

I shot back, "What you made me do, you asshole."

He shut up then and signed the paper. They let him take me home. He asked on the way to the car, "Why did you shoplift those damn chips?"

I said, "Chips, hell. I almost took the whole store. Shut up and give me the damn keys."

He didn't give them to me right away. He looked around to see who was out where the car was parked at the curb.

I said, "Give me the keys and get in the back seat. "

He did, and I drove home slowly. He let go the moment we came out of the station. He was drunk. I didn't know how he could stand up straight while he was talking to them, paying the fine, and signing me out. But he did it. I could tell he was drunker than hell by his watery eyes and the way he controlled his mouth. His whole body was kind of clutched tight, measured, while he was answering their questions.

All he said on the way home was, "Your mother sent me because she's madder than hell, and she blames me for absolutely everything."

"You are to blame and you know it."

When we got home, neither of them said anything to me. He kept on walking to their room. I knew he had to get a drink. He'd have said, "God, how I need a drink!"

You'd think with what I did, they'd be all over me. But no! I rule that house. I am just a kid, but it's like I'm their parents. As soon as I got there, looking at me cross-eyed, Mother said, "Cook for your sister."

I went in the kitchen and started cooking sausages and eggs for them. Dad came back, and they both sat and watched me like I was some goddamn miracle. My mother called my name when I was flipping the eggs. I gave them a plate of eggs and sausage and toast. She started to say something about how to serve breakfast properly. I looked at her sternly out of the corner of my eye.

She said my name again. "Leliana." Kind of soft like.

I said, "Both of you, I can't do my job with you hanging around. Go to your room, now."

She had an arm around his neck and shoulders, where he sat in the chair, turning the eggs with his fork, but not eating a thing.

"You bastard!" she said. "What are you going to say to her?"

Wiping his mouth on his sleeve, he said, "Cunt, you're her mother. What in fuck are you going to do?"

My baby sister, Scylla, pulled on the hem of Mom's dress and mumbled, "Bastard."

I nodded to them. "See what you're teaching?"

"You remember the time you broke my jaw with a bottle of vodka?" my mother said to Dad.

He put his head in his hands and didn't answer. Then he raised his head and licked his lips and looked plaintively from one of us to the other. "And I threw her," he pointed at me, "by her beautiful hair across the room like a rag doll, my rag doll." There was something akin to helpless love in his voice. It went kind of husky at, "Rag doll."

I looked at both of them and said, "How can I cook and take care of Scylla with you two bothering me?"

She lifted up the baby and placed her in my free arm. I am thinking, as always, that it's a miracle Scylla is all right the way they both drank. Somehow it was special that Mom never took a drop of liquor while she was pregnant with Scylla. She said, "Here, Leliana."

I took the child.

"Your father is a son of a bitch," she said.

"I know," I said. "Dad is an asshole. Dad, you are an asshole," I said to him.

She said, "And a bastard." And she kissed him and me.

"I told you both to go to your room," I said. "Scat."

They both got up and went.

I fed the baby. Then put her down for her nap.

They'd left their plates on the table. I took the plates to their room. They were drinking from the same glass and nuzzling each other. I watched them for a minute, then went out and lay on the couch, reading my homework papers. After a while, Mom came out and sat near my feet on the couch. She looked at me for a long while. I looked at her, and she just wagged her head and said, "I love you, Leliana."

I looked at her and told her the only news I could give. "Mom, you are drunker than hell."

She nodded. "I love you, whatever is happening."

I said, "What is this all about?"

"I just told you. Can't a mother love her daughter anymore? Your father is a son of a bitch."

"Yeah, Mom, he is an asshole. You heard me tell him so. I am already on diversion, Mom. This new shoplifting means more of that added on."

"I can't hear that now." She looked at me a while longer and added, "You're going to have your own kids one day."

"If I do, I sure in hell don't want them to be my parents. I don't want them to raise me. That's why I am not going to drink that shit and take more drugs."

"But can we agree that I love you?"

She used to hold me and say that all the time. At one time my dad was ... I remember, kind of nice, but then he became the alcoholic in our family.

When he'd come home drunk, the three of us used to fight. I mean hit and bite and scratch. Physically we'd be bleeding and sore for days. Mom was beautiful and sober until he punched her in the face. Then she started drinking with him. And I drank with both of them.

As she drank with him, he got quieter and talked more instead of fighting. I liked this verbal battle better. Even at the sacrifice of my beautiful, loving mother as I knew her. We both were thankful that he'd gone from a violent carouser to a mild drunk with a busted liver. This change had come only when she began to drink with him.

I had had enough of this shit for now. I had to do my homework.

I said, "Mom, go to your goddamn room. Now!"

She briefly squeezed me, and I smelled alcohol instead of the perfume I used to smell when I was a little kid.

Then she went to their room.

Putting It There

IT'S ALL AROUND US. We put it there by our wanting and the new ways we were making and seeing things. We saw things new and different, and we made them the way we saw them, and as a result we put it there. Some knew we were putting it there. But no one knew the effect it was causing. The important thing was seeing life different and new, and doing it the way we were living and seeing it. Everything would be better for our doing it that way. We would soon see the progress and would be happier. We were moving to a new place.

Now we are different but putting it there has not made our lives better.

Something is wrong. But it is too late to change; so many of us want to keep making it that way. It is affecting the way we think, and we cannot change our vision or our needing to do it. It is going to increase all around us, because we are needing to be doing it the way we are seeing it.

Who could stop it? Some are trying! Some are against ever looking away from it. Hal, with thick, bulging muscles, and Jen, with beautiful wild hair and soft, bubbling lips, sing and shout it at the karaoke. But among any group are the personal trainers with beards or the unshaven ones who urge when and how to breathe, when to sleep, and where to wake up, and not to do it the way the majority is doing it. It is not all different around them, so they see what is new and beginning around everyone. They tell us, but we can't stop doing it. We try diets and lights, and we hurry to set up rules. But it had already taken us over by then, and it stopped us from thinking that we should be stopping. They saw it increasing very slowly and dangerously, but being involved in doing it that way stopped us from seeing what we were doing.

We were not seeing clearly what we were doing, until we noticed that many of us lost something in our living. We lost it in the rhythm of our breathing, in the absence of our singing, in the springiness of our steps, or in the sheer open joy of meeting and smiling, or the emptiness of our eyes.

We were always wanting to be changing our feelings. No sensation was satisfying enough. We wanted it different, always. And now it was different.

Everything happened very fast. Things that were slow and leisurely moving before moved fast now, as a blur, and we were always looking and expecting things to happen that were already over. Things that seemed all clear in one way were even clearer now in another way, and some things that we'd seen clearly before escaped us totally now.

It is in our breathing and in the total flow of what is inside of us, remaking what we are made of, joining in our being so that it is us. There is no way to stop it.

We are not feeling the same, but we are adjusting to whatever is changing us. We are hot in a different way, and when cold, we are cold in a most unusual way. We are hot and cold all at once. Sounds are also different, too clear, penetrating, taking control of the you inside of you, dragging you through another part of your being to another time and place. We hear with our total selves, and we know without remembering the experience of learning. We are weary and lost deeper down in our being.

We are doing it the way we are seeing it, being in the middle of it, directly involved in it, and it is us, the whole of it. It and us are one. That unity is becoming natural.

It is all around us now, and it is ever going to be new and different, making our breathing come faster and different, forcing constant adjusting, making us try harder to gain something that is becoming more difficult, whereas before all was not ease, but easier.

From Jugum Press

Adult Fiction

Nzinga, African Warrior Queen by Moses L. Howard

Nzinga, in history and legend, is a brilliant leader during a time of violent upheaval. This fictional biography brings to life the 17th century Angolan culture in a flourishing African kingdom, now lost, where early explorers' maps of West Africa call out: "Here reigned the celebrated Queen Nzinga!"

The Sky High Road by Moses L. Howard

How to keep hope kindled for a brighter future?

Jason, a teenage soccer player in a Ugandan village, is worried about his O-levels and grieving his father's death from AIDS. His grandmother sends Jason and his sister Katura on a journey to her home village. That unwanted chore turns to catastrophe when they are enslaved as child-soldiers in the Lord's Liberation Army.

Personal Voices in History Series

A Teacher in East Africa by Moses L. Howard

Learning from the first free students in Uganda in the 1960s.

Dr. Howard describes his experiences as an African-American lecturer from Mississippi who came to spend ten years as a teacher in Uganda, beginning first as a Fulbright Scholar in 1961.

We Were Walimu Once and Young

Edited by Brooks E. Goddard

Stories from the Teachers for East Africa and Teacher Education for East Africa experience in the 1960s, describing student and village life, adventures with flora and fauna and food, and journeys to explore remote parts of East Africa.

www.jugumpress.net

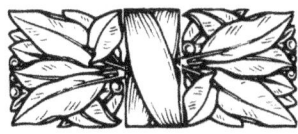

www.ingramcontent.com/pod-product-compliance
Lightning Source LLC
Chambersburg PA
CBHW070601180626
46817CB00005B/1944